BURN FOR ME

DOROTHY EWELS

ALSO BY THE AUTHOR

Links to all these books can be found on

www.dorothyewels.co.za/my-books, for all platforms

Love at Last

Destined

A Cowboy for Christmas

My Girl

Meet Me Halfway

Suspenseful Seduction World

Trusting Laurence

Liberating Mia

Cooper's Salvation

Cocky Hero Club

Sassy Surrogate

Special Forces: Operation Alpha

Operation Checkmate

Knight's Queen

Lucky in Love

Baring All

Dutch's Defense

Scooter's Endgame – releasing September 12, 2023

Gator's Gambit – releasing November 2023

Digit's Deflection – releasing January 2024

New series launching in Susan Stoker's Special Forces World 2025

Meeting Leila – *short story only available to newsletter subscribers*

Loving Leila – release date to be advised

Audio

Sassy Surrogate

*To the men and women who put their lives on the line every day,
thank you for all that you do. May He bless and keep you safe
And to the families who love and support them, thank you for your
dedication to those who give so selflessly of themselves.*
Thank you!

THE FIREMAN'S PRAYER

When I am called to duty God,
Where-ever flames may rage,
Give me strength to save some life,
Whatever be its age.

Help me embrace a little child,
Before it is too late,
Or save an older person from
The horror of that fate.

Enable me to be alert and to hear the
weakest shout,
And quickly and efficiently,
To put the fire out.

I want to fill my calling and
To give the best in me,
To guard my every neighbour and
Protect his property.

And if according to my fate,
I am to lose my life,
Please bless with your protective hand,
My children and my wife.

~ Alvin William "Smokey" Linn

THE FIREMAN'S WIFE'S PRAYER

The table's set, the meal's prepared, our guests will soon
arrive.
My husband once more disappears with a hope of keeping a
child alive.
While waiting at home alone, our plans having gone awry
My first impulse is merely to sit right down and cry.
But soon again I realize the importance of my life
When I agreed to take on the duties of being a fireman's
wife.
While there are many drawbacks, I'll take them in my stride,
Knowing "My Daddy saved a life" our children can say with
pride.
The gusting winds and raging flames may be his final fate.
But with God's help I can remain my fireman's faithful mate.

~ Author Unknown

ABOUT THIS BOOK

Katherine Spence has always dreamed of having her own speciality bakery. But her life's work is put at risk when an arsonist threatens to take it away.

Grayson James, the investigator, finds himself intrigued by the sweet baker. But he can't afford to lose focus on the case.

Tragedy strikes a match, leaving Katherine questioning the blaze in her life caused by a mad man, and the one in her heart lit by Grayson.

Can a happily ever after be plausible after the destruction in their lives? Or will Grayson and Katherine's love crumble in the heat?

A thick cloud of smoke hung low in the early morning light, a backdrop to the sparks dancing in the gentle breeze. The acrid stench of burning masked the vibrant summer scents. The sound of firemen calling to each other jarring in the quiet. Yet another iconic building, harking back to an era gone by, was lost. Nothing more than a pile of ash and dying embers.

Frustration rode Grayson James hard as he stood taking in the destruction before him. He massaged the knot of tension in his neck. It had become a permanent fixture of late. This was the third fire in a month he'd been called to in the chic suburb of Kloofnek, nestled at the foot of the majestic Table Mountain. Sitting above the bustling central business district of Cape Town, it was a much sought-after area for both work and play. Boasting a thriving business as well as an active residential community, it was the place to see and be seen.

Another beautiful day was dawning over the Mother City, and Gray took a moment to savour it. His crime scene waited for him, but he needed a moment to centre himself as he brooded over the wreckage that had once housed someone's hopes and dreams.

She put on her best face for tourists, but Cape Town in the summer months was a nightmare for firefighters. The brutal African heat mercilessly dried everything out, turning the famous African fynbos into a fire hazard. And built from all timber, the old buildings also succumbed easily to the uncaring flames.

The previous two fires, however, had turned out not to be the work of Mother Nature, but rather that of an arsonist. The same person, it seemed, since the *modus operandi* was alike in both instances. And he had a nasty suspicion today's fire would prove to be the same.

Residents and business owners alike were unhappy with the spate of fires. Gray knew he needed to close this case soon, before unhappiness turned to anger. If that happened, he knew it would only be a matter of time before people started taking matters into their own hands in a bid to protect what was theirs.

He knew he was missing something crucial; he just couldn't seem to put his finger on what it was. He was sure he'd seen something before, very similar to the recent fires in the neighbourhood. For the life of him, though, he couldn't quite place it.

Blowing out a frustrated breath, Gray surveyed the scene before him, trying to decide where best to start. The team of firefighters that had tended to the fire were in the process of packing up their gear and stowing everything back in the vehicles.

"Yo, Gray."

Gray turned towards the sound of his name, catching sight of his colleague and friend, Kyle Stevens, heading over to the nearest truck. He couldn't help but smile as he noticed the appreciative looks Kyle was getting from the ladies who had, to this point, been watching the goings-on around them.

Tall, well-muscled, and probably too good-looking for his own good, Kyle drew the attention of the ladies wherever he went. They couldn't keep their eyes off him as he strode purposefully towards his ride. Firefighting was a physically demanding job, and the guys worked hard to stay in shape. They knew it was what made the difference between life and death for them. It had to be said, though, the ladies definitely appreciated the results.

"We're all done here. Fire's out, so I've handed the building back to the owner. We're headed back to the station. I'll let you have my report this afternoon if there's no more call-outs this morning," he continued.

Walking over to intercept him, Gray replied, "Thanks Kyle. Anything I need to be aware of here?"

Kyle looked over at the smoking ruin, intense loathing crossing his handsome face. "I hate this, Gray."

"Yeah. I hear you."

Coming back to Gray's original question, Kyle added, "Nothing, other than our unsub appears to have been busy again. The signs look familiar."

Shit! Definitely not what Gray had wanted to hear. All the same, he nodded. "Thanks, Ace, I'll keep that in mind. Catch you at the station later, maybe."

Kyle gave a nod of acknowledgment and a quick wave before hopping onto the fire truck. He banged the side to let the driver know everyone was on board. Gray waved back before turning an assessing eye to the gutted building, charred and still smoking from its dousing. Pulling his notepad out of his pants pocket, Grayson took off his jacket, rolled up his sleeves, and got to work.

To preserve the integrity of his scene, he donned gloves and overshoes before making his way through the front door to start sifting through the rubble. Carefully bagging evidence as he went, he kept a lookout for the tell-tale signs that would show him not only where the fire had started but how. Kyle didn't believe this fire was an accident. Gray didn't either. His gut told him this was the work of his firebug. He just had to follow the clues.

Every fire had its own personality, like a game of chess, waiting to see who won. As he trusted his intuition to uncover the next move, skill and instinct had never steered him wrong. And they had kept him alive in this dangerous profession.

By the time he was ready to call it a day, the sun was just starting its descent. He was tired, dirty, and reeked of smoke. It had been a long day — he'd seen the sun come up, and he now got to watch the spectacular sunset as the day came to an end. He was satisfied he'd made good progress. For the first time, the arsonist had slipped up. They'd left evidence behind, giving him his first solid clue as to who it could be terrorising the neighbourhood.

Making his way over to his truck, Gray looked forward to a long, hot shower to ease his aching muscles and wash away the grime of the day. He searched for the number of his favourite pizza restaurant as he waited for his phone to pair with the car's Bluetooth system. Order placed, he contemplated a lazy evening binge watching something mindless to rest his tired brain.

Kitty wrinkled her nose as she breathed in the pungent smell of smoke that hung in the early morning air. She knew it must have been close by, but she was unprepared for the sight that greeted her as she rounded the corner onto her road. The coffee shop up the way from her own speciality bakery lay in ruin. What had once been a beautiful historical landmark was now nothing more than a heap of rubble.

She was beginning to think that maybe someone was targeting buildings in her area. Surely it couldn't be coincidence that three buildings in the same neighbourhood had burned down in such a short span of time. Maybe she should phone the local fire house and see if there was someone she could speak with to find out. It would ease her mind to have some answers.

And while she was about it, maybe she should increase her security and insurance. She definitely didn't want to be caught short. Decadence was her life as well as her livelihood. Situated on the slopes of Table Mountain, in the chic suburb of Kloofnek, the bakery was her pride and joy. She'd worked hard to achieve success in such a tough industry.

As a speciality cupcake baker, her creations where in high demand, and her business had far exceeded anything she'd dreamed she could achieve.

Katherine Spence, better known as Kitty to all, had always known she wanted to be a baker. Despite it not always having been an easy path, she loved everything about the business. Most especially the pleasure her cupcakes brought to people.

Pulling into her reserved spot in the parking lot behind her building, she hopped out of her candy-apple red Audi A3. She set the lock, steeling herself against the creepy sensation of being watched. A shiver worked its way down her spine as she dashed to the back door of the shop, unlocked it as fast as she could, and slipped inside with a sigh of relief.

Fridays were always busy days at Decadence. Saturday was party day, and she was always inundated with orders besides the usual baking that was needed for the display cases out front. As always, the day flew by in a blur of preparation, production, and clean up before heading for home. In lieu of working on Saturdays, her assistant, Jazz, worked late on Fridays to help her get all the orders filled.

Thankfully, Saturdays were short days. The shop was only open in the mornings, mainly for customers to collect their orders. Since the majority of the surrounding offices were closed on weekends, walk-in trade was minimal. With all orders already complete, the casual staff working on Saturday morning simply had to box the orders as the customers came in to collect.

In the middle of the chaos that was life on a Friday, Jazz appeared in the kitchen wearing a big grin.

"Oh my God, Kitty, the most yummy-looking man has just walked into the shop asking for you. Archie is giving him the evil eye."

"What man?" she asked as she rolled a trolley of baking tins into the industrial oven.

"He said his name is Grayson James."

"Did he say why he was looking for me?"

"No, but does it really matter why he wants to see you when he's a twelve out of ten?"

Laughing at Jazz's sassy comment, Kitty shook her head and simply replied, "Tell him I'll be out in a second. I just need to set the oven for this batch."

Giving Kitty an irreverent grin, she replied, "Will do boss-lady," and sashayed out of the kitchen.

Setting the oven and washing her hands, Kitty did a quick

mental run through to assess her progress and found herself running a little ahead. That would have meant leaving a little early that night, but her unexpected visitor had just put a spoke in that wheel. Walking into the shop area, she spotted Archie Durwood at the counter looking over the day's selection. Farther back, closer to the door, she saw her friend, Leyla Newman, sitting on a barstool at the window counter. Waiting for her, it would seem.

The three of them had gone to school together, but Archie hadn't hung out in the same circle as Kitty and Leyla. While Kitty's inherent sweetness and sunny nature had made her popular, Archie had never been able to claim the same. Being soft-hearted, she hadn't been able to bear how badly he'd been treated at school.

As if it wasn't bad enough that his parents had named him Archibald, he'd grown up to be downright plain. Insipid strawberry-blond hair, unremarkable features, and eyes too close together made it easy to overlook him in a crowd. But the clincher? Archie lisped. The kids had ragged on him mercilessly, making his life a living hell. Still, she'd been friendly and pleasant to everyone, and made no exception when it came to Archie.

Smiling, she waved at Leyla and showed her ten minutes with her hands. Layla nodded. Unfortunately, Archie happened to look up as she turned to ask Jazz where her visitor was.

A smile split Archie's face as he saw her. "Hi, Kitty. Hi. How are you today?"

"I'm fine, thank you, Archie. How are you doing?"

"I'm great, Kitty. Great. Thanks," he lisped.

"That's good, Archie. So, what can Jazz get for you today?"

"Um, you seem to be out of mocha fudge. I always have the mocha fudge. I, er, I... I, er... I don't know what else...

What else should I have?" he stammered, looking very agitated.

"I'm really sorry, Archie. I didn't realise you only ever have the mocha fudge. I'll keep that in mind. In the meantime, why don't you try the Chocolate Peppermint Delight? It's very nice with the same moist texture as the mocha fudge. It's my personal favourite."

"Oh... Oh... I didn't know that. I'll have that one then, please. So, Kitty, er..."

"I'm sorry, Archie, I don't mean to be rude, but I have someone waiting to see me. Jazz will help you. Have a lovely weekend."

Looking none too pleased, Archie glanced around, looking for the other man.

"Um, sure. Okay. You have a good weekend too."

"Jazz?" she murmured so as not to be overheard.

A mischievous grin broke out on Jazz's face, and she surreptitiously pointed to someone standing behind Kitty.

Turning, she looked towards the man standing at the far end of the counter and simply stared. Apparently, her brain felt that moment was the perfect time to quit working. Standing a good few inches over six-feet tall with sinfully handsome face, he took her breath away. Dark blond hair and emerald green eyes framed by impossibly long, thick lashes completed the whole fallen angel look.

Then he smiled. *Oh God!*

Holding out his hand, he asked, "Ms Spence? I'm Fire Marshal Grayson James of the Cape Town Fire Station. I'm investigating the fire that happened down the road. I wondered if you might have a couple of minutes to chat to me?"

Kitty forgot how to breathe. She wasn't sure if she was capable of speech either. In fact, she wasn't sure she was capable of anything besides staring. The fallen angel had a voice to match the image – deliciously husky and deep. That was not right. No man should be tall, good looking, built for sin, *and* sound like that. Not right at all!

"Hi. Yes, I'm Katherine Spence," was all she could manage at first. Mentally, she slapped herself. *For heaven's sake, get a grip.* "I'm sorry, Mr James, Fridays are really bad days for me. And my day is already spoken for tomorrow. Would Sunday do? I have an errand to run before I meet someone for breakfast, but I should be done by about one o'clock. Maybe I can meet with you around then?" she finally answered, making a valiant attempt at pulling herself together. She belatedly reached out to shake his outstretched hand. On contact, it felt like she'd touched a live wire.

"Yeah, that'll do just fine. If you can let me have your cell number, I'll give you a call to firm up the where and when," he replied.

"Oh. Sure. Just a second." Kitty went to the kitchen to retrieve a business card out of her handbag. Back in the store, she handed him the card.

"Thanks for your time. I'll be in touch." With another killer smile, he turned to leave. His walk was part saunter, part swagger, *all* sexy. *Totally not right!*

As the bell over the door chimed, Kitty snapped her mouth shut and gathered her shaken composure. She was sure she'd never encountered anybody quite like Grayson James before. Her brain re-engaging now the distraction of the super-hot fire investigator was gone, she remembered Leyla was waiting for her.

Looking around, she noticed with a sinking heart that Archie was still lurking. Thankfully, his attention was elsewhere. She headed over to where the other woman stood waiting for her.

"Hey Lee," she greeted her with a smile.

"Hey yourself, gorgeous. Who's your new friend?" Lee replied with a smile of her own, leaning in for a hug.

"Not a new friend. The local fire investigator. Apparently, he's investigating the fires we've had around here."

"So, what does he want with you?"

"Wants to interview me to see if I know anything, I guess."

"Fair enough. Well, I just popped in to see if you had a minute for some lunch, but I completely forgot it's Friday."

"Yeah. Sorry, love. I really need to get back to it. I was running a bit ahead, but that visit just set me back now." Kitty sighed. She'd really been looking forward to going home a little early and soaking in a nice hot bath.

"I'll leave you to it then. Cheers, babe. I'll chat to you later, yeah?"

"Sure. Chat then, babes."

She turned and made a quick dash for the kitchen in the hopes of avoiding Archie. She wasn't in the mood to stand and make nice with the man. Heaving a sigh of relief as she made it to the kitchen without incident, Kitty got on with the rest of her day.

Anger roiled in their gut. He had no right. No right. They wouldn't stand for it. She belonged to them, and they wouldn't tolerate it. They couldn't allow anybody to upset their plans. Everything had been running smoothly up to this point. They would just have to make sure it continued to. Nothing could be allowed to stand between them and achieving their goal. They needed to think things through.

The sharp tone of the alarm shattered the early morning silence and dragged Kitty unwillingly from a deep, dreamless sleep. She seriously loathed her early morning starts. There should be a law or something that forbade having to get up at three in the morning. It was just not natural. Reluctantly, she rolled out of bed, heading for the shower, stretching and yawning as she went.

Kitty loved to bake but hated to get up early. Her mother always laughed at the irony. Getting up at three o'clock six mornings a week amused her mother no end. She knew how much Kitty prized her sleep. But if she wanted to be successful, she needed to be ready to trade by the time she opened for her customers at seven o'clock. Even when she'd far rather still be snuggled down in dreamland.

Moving through her morning routine like an automaton, Kitty headed for the kitchen to get a cup of coffee to jumpstart her brain. On another jaw-popping yawn, she reached for her travel mug while the coffee machine gurgled its way through the brewing process. The mouth-watering smell of java permeated the air, and she smiled in anticipation of that first hit of life-giving caffeine. Having already added milk and sugar to her cup, Kitty poured the hot, fragrant coffee into it and headed for the door while taking that first, eagerly anticipated sip.

Traffic being quiet in the early morning darkness, she reviewed all that needed doing for the day. The new flavour she wanted to try out on the customers, all the special orders that needed to be filled that day, and the products she needed to get onto the shelves. Every day, she tried to keep things fresh, changing it up a bit. There were the absolute must-haves they offered daily, but she tried to rotate others to keep her customers coming back. And they certainly did. Slowly but surely, she'd built a solid reputation for excellent quality, innovative ideas, and outstanding customer service.

Her cupcakes were popular and a big hit for children's parties. But it was the fabulous special-occasion cakes she created out of the cupcakes that had become the cornerstone of her business. Especially the wedding cakes. She prided herself on being able to bring the bride's vision to life, helping to make that special day just a little bit more so.

The parking lot at the back of the bakery was deserted in the early morning hours as Kitty parked her car. Hopping out, she turned to set the alarm. Making her way to the back door of the bakery, the hair on the back of her neck stood up. That constant sense of being watched was really starting to freak her out.

*L*urking in the deepest recess, they watched as she made her way across to the door, their eyes hungrily undressing her. What they wouldn't do to have her all to themselves. *That would have to wait. They wanted everything to be perfect* *when they finally brought her home, but it wasn't yet. Soon; and they couldn't wait to show her how much they loved her.*

Engrossed so deeply in her preparation routine, Kitty started when she heard Jazz knock at the kitchen door. A quick glance at the clock told her time had flown by as she'd lost herself in the soothing rhythm of baking. Thankfully, the prep work was on target as the shop would be opening in half an hour. Jazz greeted her with a smile, making her way over to the coffee pot.

She was tiny. From her tiny feet to the top of her head covered in startlingly red hair cut super short, she resembled a pixie. But what she lacked in stature, Jazz most certainly made up for in heart. It was huge and beautiful, with a smile to match.

Returning the smile, Kitty greeted, "Good morning, Jazz. How are you doing today?"

"Hey, Kitty. Great, thanks. Gosh, it's winding up to be another scorcher of a day today." Pausing to take a sip of her coffee, she hummed in appreciation. "How are you doing?" Jazz replied.

"Great, thanks. I know, right? It looks like another aircon kind of day."

"Yeah. Oh, speaking of aircon, would it be okay if I call the refrigeration technician to come take a look at the display case on the left today? It seems to be struggling a bit in this heat."

Laughing, Kitty gave her assistant a look over her shoulder.

"Are you sure that's the only reason you want to give the technician a call?" To Kitty's amazement, Jazz blushed. "Jazz, you little flirt!" She laughed again.

"Yeah, whatever," Jazz mumbled, blushing a little more. She drank her coffee in silence for a couple of minutes before venturing, "So, would it be okay? I don't want to lose stock because it spoils."

"No problem. Just remind them to quote first. They've got a bad habit of just coming in to do the work without letting us know how much it's going to be."

"No problem." Jazz went to put her now-empty coffee cup in the sink and headed for the front of the shop. As she got to the door, Kitty called her name.

"Yeah?"

"You know I'm was only teasing about the tech, right?"

"I know."

"Thanks for being such an efficient assistant. I'd be lost without you."

Giving Kitty a sunny smile, she replied, "All part of the Jazzy service."

At exactly seven o'clock, Jazz opened the doors to a queue of people making their way to their office, looking for something to get their day started. For the next forty-five minutes, Kitty and Jazz were run off their feet. With stocks severely depleted, Kitty had just turned to head back to the kitchen for the next round of baking when the door sensor chimed and Archie walked in. He came in every day.

"Hi Kitty, hi. You're looking beautiful today, as usual," Archie lisped.

"Hi Archie. Thanks," she replied, turning to head back to the kitchen.

Jazz rolled her eyes at Kitty before turning to assist Archie.

Archie gave Jazz a creepy feeling, but she tolerated him for Kitty's sake. Kitty had been willing to give her a chance when everyone else had simply shown her the door, so she would do almost anything for her. Even putting up with the very weird and somewhat unsettling Archie Durwood.

"What's it gonna be today, Archie?" Jazz asked.

"Um, I think I'll have a mocha fudge today, please," he replied, frowning as he watched Kitty turn to leave.

"So, Kitty, I was... was, er, was wondering if you would like to have a cup of coffee with me today?" he stumbled, blushing a rather unbecoming shade of red.

Smiling through gritted teeth, Kitty turned back to him.

"Thanks, Archie, but I'm really snowed under with work today. Maybe another time," she replied.

"Oh, well, um, sure. Sure. No problem." Taking his boxed cupcake, he bowed his head. "Another time then." He headed for the door. Casting a last look over his shoulder, he left.

Jazz followed her to the kitchen. Leaning a hip against the counter, she faced Kitty. "Coffee?"

"Yes, please!" came the prompt reply.

"Man, I gotta tell you. That Archie is a right weirdo. He gives me the heebie-jeebies, pure and simple." With a shiver, she handed over the cup of coffee.

Grimacing, Kitty reached for her mug. "Jazz!"

"What?" she grinned back unrepentantly. "You can't tell me he doesn't have the same effect on you! There's something seriously off about that dude!"

Sighing, she replied, "He's always been a little... different, shall we say? His parents did him no favours with that name. And the lisp sure as hell doesn't help. Life was unbearable for him when we were at school. As he's grown older, he's gotten worse."

The doorbell on the front door chimed, saving Kitty from having to say anything more on the topic. Jazz headed for the front, and Kitty got back to work. The rest of the day whizzed by in a blur.

W ith the bakery put to rights, Kitty locked the front door. Letting herself out the back, she locked the door behind her and made her way to the car, rolling tired shoulders. A prickle of the ever-present feeling of eyes on her made its way down her spine. Looking around, she didn't see anything out of place, but the feeling wouldn't abate.

She was sure somebody was out there in the dark recesses somewhere, watching her. Her imagination ran wild as fear gripped her. She disliked feeling this way. Rushing over to her car, Kitty fumbled with the fob to unlock, scrambling into the safety of the interior when she finally managed to get it open. She slammed the door and locked it, glanced around one last time before starting the engine.

To distract herself from the dread, she connected her phone to the car's Bluetooth system. First, she dialled her friend Morgan's number. When she got no answer, she dialled Lee's number. While she waited for her to answer, Kitty started the car and pulled out of the parking lot. She couldn't wait to get home.

"Hey gorgeous. How goes?" Lee answered.

"Hi yourself. Just headed for home, so I thought I'd check in. How's your day been?"

The mindless chatter helped calm her jangling nerves and made the drive home more palatable.

Summertime traffic was the worst, especially over the weekends. Everybody was either headed for the beach to enjoy the sun or the mall to enjoy the air conditioning. Eventually, Kitty pulled into her parking space at home, heaving a sigh of relief. Sitting bumper to bumper scarcely moving for kilometres on end wasn't her favourite way to spend her time. It had been a long day, but nothing that a hot soak, a good book, and a glass of wine couldn't cure. Not necessarily in that order. And at least she'd had Leyla's rapier wit to keep her company on the irritating drive.

Usually Kitty came home earlier in the day, but today she'd stayed until closing so she could try out some new ideas. So, she was definitely looking forward to relaxing.

Life, it seemed, had other ideas, as the downstairs buzzer sounded. It looked like her much-anticipated soak wasn't to be.

"Hello?" she said.

"Hi, open up," a voice replied.

Smiling, she pressed the door release to let Morgan Preston in. Their mothers were childhood friends. Even after getting married and having children of their own, their friendship had endured. And, of course, they were thrilled when their girls had become best friends almost since birth. Kitty stood by the open door waiting for the lift to arrive.

"Hiya, precious. I saw you were looking for me earlier, so I thought I'd pop by. How was your day?" Morgan queried as she made her way into the apartment.

"Crazy busy, but good. Yours?" Kitty reached out to give Morgan a big hug.

"Urgh! The day from hell. Somehow, the dick managed to corrupt the document file he needs for a meeting on

Monday, and guess who has to ride to the rescue yet again? And on a Saturday," she pouted. Throwing herself down on the nearest sofa, she continued, "I don't get paid enough for this crap. Even the side benefits don't make up for that frustration."

Kitty laughed at her friend.

"Don't let Greg hear you calling him a dick!" she teased, referring to Morgan's boss.

"I'm not sure what the hell I was thinking going to work for him. God, he's a terrible boss."

"Come on, Morgs. Surely he can't be that bad."

"Yes. Yes, he can. And he is," Morgan replied before continuing. "How about a super big glass of wine to unwind?" She grinned hopefully.

Shaking her head at her friend, Kitty replied, "My thoughts exactly. I had intended to have that super big glass of wine in the bath, but since you've nixed that idea, what did you have in mind?"

"A nice girly night in with lots of that wine? Greg's out tonight, so I thought we could just hang out. I miss our girl time."

Something in Morgan's tone didn't quite sit right, and Kitty tried to get a read on her without making it obvious. She and her boss, Greg, had gotten together one night while out of town on business, but theirs had not been an easy relationship.

There was a vulnerable light in Morgan's eyes that Kitty didn't like. It was so unlike her. Kitty had tried to warn Morgan that getting involved with her married boss was not a good idea. She had worried about an eventuality like this. Unfortunately, Morgan caught her look. Her eyes shuttered immediately, and she smiled.

Not wanting to upset her friend by pressing, Kitty simply replied, "Sounds like a perfect evening."

She headed for the kitchen to grab the wine and glasses.

"Archie came into the shop again today," she called over her shoulder. "I really don't know what to do about him anymore. He creeps poor Jazz out, and I've got to agree, he makes me pretty uncomfortable too. But I really can't find it in my heart to ban him from the shop. He's a paying customer."

Morgan looked over at Kitty as she came back into the room. "You're far too soft for your own good. You know that, right?"

Sighing, she couldn't help but agree with her friend. "I know. But to be fair, he hasn't done anything untoward. Other than to constantly ask me out for a cup of coffee, he's done nothing to warrant me banning him. I just wish he'd stop asking me to go out with him. I don't know how to cut him off without hurting his feelings."

"Yeah, sorry to break it to you, precious, but this is destined to not end well. There's no way to avoid hurting his feelings. Wouldn't it be better to just make it a clean break?"

"Urgh! I know you're right, but I just can't. I don't have it in me." Pouring them each a glass of wine, Kitty passed one over. "Chin, chin, darling."

Morgan tapped her glass gently against Kitty's. "Bottom's up, babes." Her smile finally reaching her eyes, she took a big sip. "So, what's new, newsy, and exciting in your life?"

"I met the hottest guy on the face of planet Earth."

"What? You sly devil! Why am I only hearing about this now?"

Kitty laughed at her friend.

"Because our lives have been crazy busy? And it only happened yesterday," she replied.

"I guess you're right." Morgan nodded. "So? Spill, girlfriend. Tell me all about McHottie."

"Oh God, Morgs, I must have come across as the lamest

bimbo ever. I got one look at him and my brain stalled. I'm just grateful I wasn't drooling." Kitty buried her face in her hands, feeling it heat up.

"You? At a loss for words? Never!" Morgan chuckled. "I would have paid good money to see that."

"Yup. Me. It was so embarrassing. And now I have to meet up with him again about the recent spate of fires in the area," she mumbled through her hands.

"Ooh. There's potential here, methinks."

Tossing a scatter cushion at Morgan, Kitty reached for her glass, laughing. "Only you would think like that. Now, what are we going to do about food?"

The rest of the evening sped by as they joked around, enjoying each other's company. But Kitty kept a close eye on her friend. All was not well with Morgan, she suspected. And she didn't like it. Not one bit.

The excitement was overwhelming. It was all they could do to contain themselves. Everything was in place for their next target. It wouldn't take much to get it done, and it would be one less for her to worry about. She would realise how much she loved them when she understood that they were doing all of this for her. There was nothing they wouldn't do for her. Staring at all the photos on the wall, they smiled. Soon, my love. We'll be together soon, as we've always been meant to be. They stroked a loving hand over the photo nearest to them, their eyes gleaming with madness. The madness that consumed them a little more every day.

CHAPTER 3

The sounds of Nickelback filled her apartment's kitchen as Kitty was drying her hands, ringing coming from her handbag. Everything had been put to rights, and she was about to head out the door. She was on her way to drop off cupcakes at Nazareth House.

Kitty loved doing her bit for the inhabitants of the home. An organisation steeped in history, their aim since 1881 was to look after the indigent, elderly, and orphaned children. They offered a comfortable home and nursing to those in need. It warmed her heart to see the enjoyment her cupcakes brought to those who lived there, bringing a little bit of sunshine into their lives.

Finally, she managed to dig her phone out of her bag.

"Hello?"

"Ms Spence, Grayson James. I'm calling to confirm a time and place with you for our meeting this afternoon."

"Hi, Mr James, yes. I'm just about to leave. I make a delivery to Nazareth House every week and then treat the sisters to breakfast at a lovely little coffee shop down the road from them — the Red Velvet Lounge. How about we meet there around one o'clock?"

"Great. I know of the place. I'll see you there."

***

The nuns had left a few minutes earlier, and Kitty called for another cup of coffee as she sat waiting for the sinfully gorgeous Grayson James. She couldn't remember a time that a man had piqued her interest like he did. It seemed like forever ago since a man had made her skin tingle and her belly flutter.

***

Bold as brass and larger than life, Grayson strolled in right on time. He looked around and spotted her sitting at a window table. Taking a moment to absorb the sight of her, he felt rooted to the spot. She was quite possibly the most beautiful woman he'd ever seen, with her raven tresses tumbling haphazardly down her back and dimpled smile.

Walking over to the table, surprisingly, she stood when he reached her, holding out her hand to shake. At around five-foot-two, she wasn't the tallest woman he'd ever been attracted to, but she certainly had magnificent curves in all the right places, packing quite the visual punch.

Grayson said, "Ms Spence. Thank you for taking the time to meet with me. May I?" he indicated the chair opposite her.

"Yes, of course. It's a pleasure, Mr James."

"Please, call me Gray."

"Oh, well, thank you. Gray then. And please, call me Kitty," she replied, her soulful eyes the colour of jade and amber lighting up, pouty bee-stung lips lifting, and a heart-shaped face boasting the most adorable dimple when she smiled.

He needed to get his head back in the game. Since when did he wax lyrical about anything, let alone a woman? It just wasn't him. He was here on business, not looking for his soul mate. *Whoa there. Where the hell had that thought come from? Pull it together, man. Go do what you came to do, then get the hell out of dodge.*

"Thanks," he acknowledged with a grin of his own.

"So, what can I do for you, Mr – sorry, Gray?"

For a moment, Gray's mind wandered into dangerous territory as he looked at her lips. Clearing his throat, he chided himself silently. *Not cool, dude. Pull your shit together.*

"As I mentioned on Friday, I'm investigating the recent fires in Kloofnek."

"Gosh, yes. Terrible! My heart aches for those poor people. I have no idea what I would do if it happened to me. My shop means everything to me."

"I was wondering if you might have any information that could shed some light on the case."

"I really don't think so. I can't honestly say that I've seen or heard anything out of the ordinary."

"Well, let's go through the list of questions I have and see where that gets us. Okay?"

"Okay," Kitty agreed.

Gray asked his questions, and Kitty answered as best she could. Eventually, he decided he'd gotten about all he was going to get about the fires. Completely forgetting his intentions of only interviewing the delectable Kitty Spence and getting the hell out, he turned his attention to asking questions of a different kind.

She really piqued his interest. He sensed there was a lot more to the woman than she showed the world. And damned if he didn't want to unearth all that she concealed. Turning loose one of his killer smiles, he leaned in and asked, "So tell me, Kitty, is there a Mr Kitty waiting at home for you?"

Dimple showing, distracting him from his train of thought for a second, she replied, "Wow, you certainly don't beat around the bush, do you?"

Giving an unrepentant shrug, he replied, "I've never seen the point of it. Besides, life's too short. In my profession, you can't afford to waste a second. You never know when your time is up."

"I guess I can see your point. I'm just not used to going at a million miles an hour. But okay, I'll play." Taking a moment to drink the last of her coffee, Kitty eyed him over the top of her cup. When she was done, she set the cup back in its saucer and replied, "No, there is no Mr Kitty waiting for me at home, or anywhere else for that matter."

Gray first felt surprise and then delight at the fact that she was single. It seemed the gods were smiling down on him of late.

His rather delightful meeting with Kitty Spence long over, Gray had been back at it for hours. Much as he'd wanted to linger over coffee getting to know her better, he'd headed back to the fire station instead and gone over every bit of evidence he'd found. Again. He'd read and re-read the reports. Over and over, until his eyes blurred. What was he missing? Something seemed off at the point of origin. The pattern was unusual – not the run-of-the-mill accelerant pattern. He just couldn't put his finger on it, but he knew it was something important.

Whatever it was that he was missing, he knew it was the key to solving the spate of fires in Kloofnek. And he was sure it was hiding in plain sight. He'd thought the evidence he'd found at the last scene would give more insight into the perpetrator, but still he had nothing. Running his hands through his hair in utter frustration, he got up to get another cup of coffee.

The fire house was quiet in the early hours of the morning. Everyone getting in a bit of sleep while they could. He enjoyed working in those quiet hours. It helped him to focus. Not that it seemed to be helping at the moment.

The sudden jangle of the klaxon was loud and out of place in the silence. And just as suddenly, the fire house came to life. Firefighters and paramedics alike headed for their vehicles to respond to the call. As one of the firefighters ran past him, he asked where the fire was.

"High up on Kloof Street somewhere," came the response.

Gray's stomach sank. Damn it, he was too late. The arsonist had struck again before he could figure it all out. Someone had just lost their business because he couldn't nail this one down. Grabbing his gear, he headed for the fire scene.

Chaos reigned. Pulling up to the scene, Gray turned his car off and sat looking at it. People were standing all over the place, jostling each other to gawk at the spectacle. Flames reached high in the night sky, lighting the area up like daylight. Fire trucks and rescue vehicles crammed into the narrow street, adding to the general sense of bedlam. To add insult to injury, there were reporters and news crews everywhere.

Gritting his teeth, he got out of the car and headed for the nearest policeman.

Showing the man his ID, he asked, "Evening, officer. Who is in charge here?"

Turning to look at him, the officer replied, "Evening, sir. Sergeant Monroe, over there." The officer pointed to an older gentleman standing talking to one of his uniforms.

"Thank you."

He made his way over to the two men, irritation stiffening his shoulders. Again, he showed his credentials.

"Gentlemen, sorry for interrupting, but I need a word with you, Sergeant Monroe, if you don't mind."

"Sure," Monroe replied. Speaking to his officer, he continued, "Give me a second?"

The officer nodded and moved a short distance away.

"What can I do for you, young man?"

Extending his hand to Sergeant Monroe, Gray said, "Fire Marshal Grayson James. I'm the investigator for the Cape Town Fire Station."

"Nice to meet you, Mr James. What can I do for you?"

"Apparently, the public has absolutely no concept of self-preservation, Sergeant. I would be very grateful if you could please push the safety barrier back farther to keep the public safe, especially from themselves. Also, I would greatly appreciate it if you could keep the press as far away from the scene as you can manage. Otherwise, they badger my guys and generally just get in everyone's way."

"You've got it, son. I'll see to it. Bloody press slither in everywhere they're not wanted."

"Appreciate it, sir." As the Sergeant turned to carry out his requests, Gray briefly allowed his head to bow as he gathered himself.

Heading over to the nearest truck, he spotted the senior officer on site. Jeffrey Erickson was a seasoned member of the fire department, and he enjoyed working with him.

"Jeff," he greeted the other gentleman, "what have you got for me?"

"Hey, Gray. Man, this one is putting up one hell of a fight. My boys are battling to put her down." He shook his head sadly. "I've been at this game for a lot of years and pretty much seen them all. I'm going to go out on a limb here and call this one arson too."

Just then a shout went up. Turning to see what the problem was, they were in time to see the building collapse in on itself. Jeff's radio crackled to life.

"Sir, we've got a man down in the building. Matthews and Simms went in for search and rescue, but only Simms got out before she fell. Shit, sir, Matthews is still in there."

Cursing ripely, Erikson barked into his radio, "Ensure the building is stable enough to send someone in after him. If it's a go, send Collins and Wilkes in. They've got the most experience on the team. Get him out. Go. Go!"

They'd known that he would be a problem from the time they'd first laid eyes on him. The fire investigator was going to ruin everything, and they couldn't let that happen. They knew she was theirs. They'd just needed to give her the time and space to realise it, but he'd changed the game. They'd have to move their schedule up to win over their girl.

Let that be a lesson to you, Mr Fire Investigator. If you don't stay away from her, you're next. She will *be ours. We will not tolerate your interference. She is ours! She always has been. You're ruining everything with your misplaced arrogant sense of superiority. Not that it's helped you any. You still haven't figured it out, have you? That's because we're better than you.*

CHAPTER 4

Rolling his tired shoulders, Gray stood surveying the destruction. Smouldering rubble and shattered dreams lay all around him. He was just grateful they'd managed to rescue their colleague who had been trapped when the building had collapsed. He'd known Matthews since the man had come on board as a raw rookie nine years ago. He prayed the man made it through.

There were dark parts to the job, but few were darker than losing a firefighter on duty. Having to tell a wife, husband, or parent their loved one wasn't coming home was something he never wanted to do. He was grateful that wasn't part of his job description, and he certainly didn't envy the chaplain his position. He felt so powerless at times like this, knowing he couldn't change the outcome for Matthews. What he could do was find the answers and get justice for his colleague, his friend.

He'd have to wait for the heat to disperse before he could start sifting through the debris, and he desperately needed a cup of coffee. There was time for a quick visit to the hospital to update himself on Matthews' condition and then he'd come back and get to work finding the answers he needed to nail this bastard.

Suddenly, he had an overwhelming urge to see Kitty. It had been a crappy morning so far, and he felt a deep need to go to her. Just to be in her presence. Just to talk to her about nothing of consequence. Just to soak her in.

What was it about this woman that had him so enthralled? He couldn't put his finger on it, but there was something powerful that drew him in, made him want to be with her, around her. When she smiled, it was like the sun coming out on a gloomy day. Gray had never been the romantic type. He wasn't prone to flowery thoughts about love, and he'd certainly never felt the need to find "the one". But Kitty's appearance in his life had the impact of a meteor crashing to earth.

Kitty and coffee – now there was a thought. Deciding that's what he would do, Gray headed for his truck.

As he pulled into the parking lot behind Decadence, he checked the time. Seeing it was not quite three thirty a.m. he realised she might not be there yet. He decided he'd check, and if she wasn't there, he'd wait for her; so he headed over to the back door. When he got no answer to his knock, Gray made himself comfortable against the door frame and hoped he wouldn't have to wait too long.

Rewarded for his patience not ten minutes later, he saw Kitty pull into the lot. She got out of her vehicle, locked it, and looked around her before striding quickly his way. He watched, and he enjoyed what he saw.

What the hell? Kitty did a double-take. *Had someone been standing over by the dumpster?*

That feeling she was being watched raced up her spine again, raising every hair on her body. It was really starting to freak her out. She was so sick of feeling like this every time she came to work — to the point she was toying with the idea of hiring a security guard for the parking lot. Maybe her neighbours would be willing to share the expense. With all the fires that had happened in their immediate vicinity, she was sure they would be happy to. Dashing to the door, she was so deep in thought she didn't see the man standing in the doorway of her shop.

Looking up to insert her key in the lock, she started violently as she spotted Gray lounging against her door.

"Wow, Gray!" she exclaimed as she clapped a hand over her galloping heart. "You scared the hell out of me."

"Sorry, I didn't mean to. You seemed so far away. Everything all right?"

She chewed on her lower lip, briefly mulling over whether she should share her suspicions. His eyes followed the movement, and Kitty saw them warm. Feeling a little flustered at the look, she motioned toward the door.

"Come on in. Let's chat inside."

He stepped out of her way so she could unlock the door and followed her in.

As she filled the coffee machine's tank with water, Kitty tried to arrange her thoughts. She got mugs out of the cupboard, ready to pour the coffee. Turning to speak, she bumped into a solid body. Looking up at him, she licked her lips. She saw his eyes on her mouth, watched them darken.

"Sorry, I didn't expect you to be standing there."

Smiling apologetically, he took a step back.

"Are you okay? Something seems to have you pretty jumpy."

Taking a deep breath, she admitted, "I think someone is watching me."

"*What?* Have you been to the police?"

Kitty shook her head. "No, I don't have anything concrete. I just get this really creepy feeling. Every morning when I get to work and again in the evening when I leave, I get the sense someone is watching me come and go. I don't have any solid evidence. Maybe I just have an overactive imagination. But it's really starting to get to me."

"Honey, I may only have known you a short time, but you definitely don't come across as the flighty, high-strung kind of woman who would imagine things like that."

Blushing, she turned to pour the coffee, now finished brewing, to give herself a minute to collect her composure. His endearment had delivered a heady punch to her feminine senses. She had no idea what it was about him, but Gray made her want things she hadn't in the longest time. With just a look or a smile, he made her hot and needy. She wanted him in the worst way.

Handing him a mug, she pushed the sugar over to him and headed over to the fridge for the milk.

"So Gray, what brings you to my door so early in the morning? Wait, is that smoke I smell?" Her brain finally catching up with the rest of her, she'd just noticed a strong scent of smoke when she was near to him.

With a grim set to his beautiful face, he nodded.

"I've just come from the scene of a fire up the road." His sigh seemed to come from his soul.

"Oh. Are *you* okay?"

"It's been a bitch of a morning. The building collapsed, and one of our guys couldn't get out in time. They got him out, but he's in critical condition. I'm headed home to shower so I can pop in at the hospital before I get started on processing the scene." Pausing, he seemed to debate whether to continue before he finally said, "I just wanted to see you before I go home. Needed to see you." Leaning into her space, Gray's eyes moved over her face, intense and so very green. He went on. "I'm drawn to you, to be with you. Why do you think that is, Kitty?"

Her eyes went big, and her lips parted in surprise, but no words came out.

"There's so much that needs to be done, and all I can think about is you. What you sound like when you wake up in the morning, what you do in your spare time, what you taste like, what you sound like when you come. And yet I barely know you."

She couldn't seem to catch her breath. His words evoked a slow burn in her. Still, she said nothing. Just looked up into his beautiful eyes and got lost there, in his intensity.

"Kitty..."

Nervously chewing on her lower lip, she looked up at him. "Yes, Gray?"

"Can I see you sometime?"

"You mean like a date?" She barely dared to breathe as he leaned in a little closer.

"Yeah. Like a date." Reaching out, he wrapped a hand around the back of her neck and slowly drew her in. Lowering his head until his forehead rested against hers, he smiled. "Kitty?"

"Yes, Gray?"

"I'm going to kiss you now."

Looking up at him with huge eyes, she nodded.

As he touched his lips to hers, Kitty felt it throughout her whole body. Lust sparked, and she heard Gray groan as he drew her tighter against him, deepening the kiss.

The ringing of his cell phone intruded. Breaking off the embrace, he reached for his phone.

"James." He listened intently as the person on the other side spoke rapidly and then, "Yes, chief. I'll be there in forty-five minutes." With a look of what appeared to be regret, he drew her in for one last hug. "I have to go, but this isn't over. I'll call you soon."

The look he gave her before turning to leave scorched all the way to her core.

———

T*he madness was consuming them a little more every day. Standing in the dark recess out of sight, their body bristled with rage. This man wouldn't go away.*

What do we have to do to get rid of you? Why won't you stay away from what's ours? Don't you understand? She has always been ours. We can't allow you to come between us. You leave us no choice. We will have to move our plans up now. And it'll be your fault.

CHAPTER 5

Wedding season was hitting hard this year, and the orders were flooding in for Kitty's speciality wedding cakes created with cupcakes. Her hours were long, and there wasn't much time for anything. She was absolutely thrilled that all her hard work was paying huge dividends this year with the increase in business.

Yet she still found herself thinking of the very sexy fire marshal at the oddest moments. But mostly when she was engaged in the soothing, mindless task of icing and decorating cupcakes. Where was he? What was he doing? Was he safe? Did he think of her?

Taking a moment, she stepped back from the design she was working on to get a look at how it was shaping up. The bride had requested a traditional wedding cake with a peacock as a feature instead of the usual flowers and ribbon. Happy with how it was turning out, she went back to icing and decorating to create the vibrant blue plumage of the bird.

The ringing of her cell phone broke the rhythm she had

going. Irritated at the interruption, she wiped her hands and rummaged around in her handbag to find the offending instrument. Her fingers finally feeling it in the bottom, she whipped it out to answer before it rang off.

"Hello?"

"Hi, Kitty?"

She'd recognise that voice anywhere, and just the sound of it had her knees going weak. She couldn't believe it was Gray calling since she had been daydreaming about him as she worked. It was like she'd conjured him up with the power of thought alone. Laughing at her whimsy, she answered, "Yes. Hi Gray."

"Am I interrupting anything, or do you have a minute to chat?"

"I'm busy icing a wedding cake, but I've got a minute. What's up?"

"Ah. I won't keep you too long then. I'd really like to see you again. I thought I'd take you out to dinner, if you're free."

Surprised at the girlish excitement that coursed through her, Kitty took a second before replying, "Sure, dinner sounds great. What did you have in mind?"

Not directly answering the question, Gray replied, "How about I pick you up at seven tomorrow evening? There's a really nice place in Green Point I'd like to take you to."

"That sounds rather mysterious. Is it meant to be a surprise?"

"Yes ma'am. I'll see you at seven tomorrow."

"At least tell me what the dress code is?"

"Their dress code is smart to formal. I'll leave you to decide how best to interpret that. And on that note, I'll say goodbye so you can get back to creating your magic."

"Yeah, I guess this wedding cake isn't going to make itself." Kitty laughed. "See you tomorrow then."

"I look forward to it," Gray replied, his voice taking on a huskier note than usual. "See you."

The phone went dead in her ear, and Kitty returned it to her handbag. But she didn't get back to her task immediately. Her thoughts were still on the conversation she'd just had with Gray.

When he'd said he'd phone her soon, she thought he'd said it just for something to say. Clearly, he had meant it. And she was glad he had. Kitty was excited to see the sexy fire marshal again. Going back to her icing and decorating, her thoughts still focused on the following evening.

Kitty mentally flicked through the contents of her wardrobe, and her heart sank as she came to the conclusion that she had nothing suitable for her date with Gray. Her only solution was to call up her girlfriends and go shopping that evening after work. After digging her cell phone back out of her bag, she called first Morgan and then Lee, thankful that a nearby mall only closed at nine in the evening. She just prayed it would be enough time to find the perfect outfit.

Pulling into a parking bay, Kitty looked around to see if she could see her girlfriends. Not seeing either of them, she climbed out of her car, hitting the lock button on the key fob as she headed into the shopping centre. They'd probably be waiting for her at the designated spot.

She was looking forward to some girl time. It had been an age since the three of them had hung out shopping, eating, chatting, and enjoying each other's company. And there was nobody who could find the perfect outfit like Morgan.

Locating them in front of the first shop they'd decided on, Kitty hugged her friends.

"All right, precious. What's the brief? What look are we going for?" Morgan asked.

"I have no idea where we're going other than it's in Green Point and there's a dress code of smart to formal."

"Ooh, fancy," Lee chimed in.

"Yeah, tell me about it. Apparently, it's a secret where we're going. Not overly helpful though, right?"

"Green Point, you say?" Morgan asked.

"Yes. That's all I know other than the dress code I've told you," Kitty replied, pulling a face.

Morgan gave her a sly smile before saying, "If it's the place I think it is, then, girlfriend, he's going all out to impress. Right. Let's go spend some of that hard-earned cash of yours, precious. Mama's got a plan."

Kitty groaned out loud. Her credit card in Morgan's hands gave her nightmares.

Both Lee and Morgan laughed at her.

"Don't be such a baby. It's not *that* bad," Lee managed through her laughter.

"Easy for you to say. It's not your credit card about to be laid to waste by the Mistress of Shopping." Kitty grimaced, causing the other two to laugh again.

"Oh, come on. I'm not that bad!" Morgan interjected.

As one, Kitty and Lee replied, "Yes, you are."

On another laugh, the three of them entered the store and got down to the serious business of finding the perfect outfit.

Two hours, thirty outfits tried and denied, and four shops later, Kitty wanted to choke Morgan as only a best friend could. With only two stores remaining, Kitty was also about to call the whole thing off. Her feet were starting to hurt, and she was starving. They'd seen so many lovely things, none of which Morgan had deemed "perfect". So, they'd kept searching. But now she was tired of trying clothes on.

"Come on, precious. We've only got two more boutiques," Morgan cajoled, seeing the mutinous look on Kitty's face.

Kitty looked to Lee for support. The other woman just shrugged her shoulders. They both knew what Morgan was like when it came to clothes shopping.

"Fine. Let's do this. The quicker we get done, the sooner we can eat. I'm starving."

They were barely through the door when Morgan made a humming sound in the back of her throat and shot off like a greyhound after prey.

"This is *it*! I told you we'd find it. You're going to knock the fire inspector's feet right out from under him. Girlfriend, you are going to be *smoking hot* in this. He's not going to know what hit him." Morgan grinned over at Kitty, holding an almost indecently sexy little black dress in her hand.

The skirt was short and fitted and would cling lovingly to every curve, and it had a slouched top with a halter-neck collar. But the clincher was the back. Or rather the lack thereof. Gold chains crisscrossed to hold the sides together. Kitty fell in love instantly.

"Well? Don't just stand there staring at it. Go try it on. We want to see how it looks on you," Morgan prompted.

Taking the dress, Kitty headed for the changing rooms. Once it was on, she took a moment to appreciate how good the dress looked before opening the door to show the others.

"Oh my God, the poor man isn't going to know what hit him when he gets a load of you in that dress, babes," Morgan exclaimed, her eyes gleaming with excitement for her friend.

Kitty looked over at Lee. "So, what do you think?" she asked, wondering at the funny look on the other woman's face.

The moment Kitty spoke to her, the look disappeared from her face. Lee smiled, taking a moment to reply, "You look amazing. He's a lucky guy."

"Well, Morgs, I've got to say, you've done it again. I love it. Now let's get shoes and a clutch and get the hell out. I'm starving."

P ulling into the parking lot, he'd found the spot she'd told him to park in. Hopping out, he took in the layout of the complex. Having arrived a couple minutes early, Gray waited until exactly seven to ring the bell at the security gate to Kitty's complex. A moment later, he heard her answer.

"Yes?"

"Hi, it's Gray."

"Hi Gray. Come on up."

He headed up to her first-floor apartment, foregoing the lift and taking the stairs instead. Reaching her door, he knocked then turned to take in the magnificent view of Table Bay at night from the walkway that ran past the front of her apartment. He heard the door open behind him. Taking one last look at the view, he turned toward the open door and froze.

He was sure his brain short-circuited because he could do nothing more than stand and stare at the vision in front of him. Killer black dress, killer heels, and killer curves, all wrapped in one perfect package. How the hell was a man supposed to think?

Slowly, his eyes travelled from the tip of her head to the tip of her toes. He swallowed. Hard. Returning his gaze to hers, he felt the slow burn of desire. Not wanting to scare her off before they even left, Gray belatedly held out the bunch of pure white carnations he'd brought her.

Finally finding his voice, he said, "Hi there." His words

came out huskier than usual, so he cleared his throat before continuing. "These are for you."

She smiled, showing him her dimple. Reaching out a graceful hand, she took the flowers from him.

"Hi. Thank you so much. These are absolutely beautiful. Let me just pop these in some water and we can get going."

When she turned on her heel to go put the flowers in water, he felt his jaw drop open. There was absolutely no back to the dress. Just some gold chain criss-crossing the expanse of smooth, unmarred skin of her back. *Well, damn!*

Keep it together, Gray! Cool, stay cool. Deciding it was best he didn't follow her into the apartment, he called after her, "I'll just wait out here for you then."

"No problem. I'll just be a minute," she replied.

In no time, she was back. She locked her apartment and turned to him. Putting a hand to the small of her back, he led her over to the lift. His hand seemed to almost burn where it touched the skin of her bare back. He bit back a groan. It was going to be a long night.

Usually, Gray had no problem showing the ladies how he felt, but there was something special about Kitty. She wasn't his usual one-night stand or short-term, no-strings attached hook-up. He tamped down his baser desires and focused on what she was saying.

"Sorry, I missed that. Say again?"

Kitty turned her head to look at him. Instead of repeating herself, she said, "Is everything okay, Gray? You seem a little distracted."

Biting back a snort, he smiled down at her. There was no way in hell he was confessing to her that she had him tied up in knots. And it wasn't a feeling he was used to. He was used to being the one who did the knot-tying.

"Sorry I seem a little distracted. This Kloofnek case has me a little out of sorts. Otherwise, all good. No problems."

It was only a partial untruth. The case did have him out of sorts. Just not right that second. That was one hundred percent all the delectable Ms Spence.

"Is there a problem with the case?"

"Let's not talk about the case, shall we? Let's just focus on having a good evening, yeah?"

"Sounds like a good idea." Kitty smiled. "Where are we going?"

"It's a surprise."

Stepping out of the lift, Gray guided her over to his car. Unlocking the car with the fob as they approached, he opened the passenger door and handed her down into her seat. He closed the door and headed around the hood to the driver's side.

"Dessert for the lady?" The waiter asked, giving Kitty a toothy smile as he removed her dinner plate.

Gray frowned, not at all pleased the man had subtly been hitting on Kitty all through dinner.

"Oh goodness, not right this second, thank you. Dinner was absolutely wonderful, but I need to let my food settle a bit."

"And for sir?" His far more dialled-down smile disappeared completely when he caught the look on Gray's face.

"Not right now, thank you. We'll let you know when we're ready."

Dipping his head in acknowledgement, he left with their dinner dishes.

Turning his attention back to Kitty, he saw her looking over at the band. They were busy tuning their instruments in readiness for their set. Leaning back in his chair, he studied her. She was exquisite. She had her hair up in some complicated-looking updo that showed off her graceful neck and showcased her beautiful face.

She'd done something smoky with her eye makeup that made her big eyes seem impossibly larger. Siren-red lipstick rounded out a look that was guaranteed to bring a man to his knees.

"Is that a dance floor in front of the band?" She turned her head to look at him as she spoke.

"Yeah, it is. One of the reasons I love coming here. They play jazz, swing, and salsa music here, and you're invited to dance if the mood grabs you."

A look of surprise crossed her face. "You dance?"

"Sure. I love to. My mom taught me from a young age. She believed men should know how to cook, clean, and dance."

"Sounds like your mom's a really smart lady."

"That she was," he replied.

At his words, Kitty leaned forward, resting her chin on a palm. The look she gave him seemed to see all the way into him. Gray shifted uncomfortably. It almost seemed like she saw too much.

"Was?" was all she said though.

He nodded. "My mom passed a few years ago."

"Oh, Gray, I'm so sorry."

Just then a voice announced that the band was about to start and diners were welcome to dance. Conversation ceased for the moment as Gray and Kitty sat listening for a few minutes. After a short while, Gray leaned closer so she'd hear him over the music.

"Do you dance, Kitty?"

"Yes. Like you, I love to dance. My mom used to take me for ballroom and Latin American dance lessons as a child.

And as an adult, I've taken random classes. You know, like line dancing, swing, and such."

"So, tell me, do you salsa?"

"I haven't in ages. I'm not sure I'd remember how to."

"Come on. Let's see if I can jog your memory."

Gray couldn't wait to get her out on to the dance floor. He wanted those curves pressed up close. He just hoped he'd survive. Taking their place on the floor amongst the handful of other brave souls, she placed her soft hand in his. Pulling her in closer, he placed his other hand on the smooth expanse of her back. That slow burn flared a little higher.

Gray expertly led Kitty into the salsa as the band started a new tune. A little stiff at first, she slowly relaxed in his grip as they found their rhythm, immersing themselves in the sensual beat. Confident and sure in his lead, he put her through her paces. They twisted, turned, and spun in perfect sync.

When he inserted a thigh between hers and dropped her into a back bend, he felt himself tighten. He could feel her heat as she straddled his thigh, moving her torso sensually in time to the beat. As she pulled out of the dip he had her in, he took in her flushed cheeks and the way her dark eyes sparkled up at him. Good to know he wasn't the only one affected. When the salsa came to an end, the band slowed it down to give the dancers a chance to catch their breaths. Gray took the opportunity to pull Kitty closer, savouring the feel of her in his arms.

Tucking her close to his body, he rested his chin on top of her head. He just needed a moment to calm the desire raging in his bloodstream. He couldn't remember a time a woman made him feel the way Kitty did. When he felt her fingers slide into the hair at his nape, he knew he was fighting a losing battle.

H urt, rage, betrayal all bubbled into an ugly concoction of revenge. Hadn't they done this all for that ungrateful bitch? And how did she repay them? By rubbing herself all over that fucking fire inspector. What were they to do? What she was doing was unforgivable. There would have to be consequences. They needed to think. Unaware of the tears of hurt and anger that ran down their face, they continued to rock back and forth, contemplating how best to exact revenge.

CHAPTER 6

Blowing out a breath, Gray swung his office chair around to face the window, his gaze seeking out Table Mountain. Taking the sight in, he let his mind wander. It had been a long time since a case had him so stumped, but this one was proving to be a difficult one.

What had him most irritated, though, was that he recognised the work. He knew he'd encountered it before. He just couldn't figure out where. Was it one of his own cases, or had it been a case study from his training? If he could only remember, then he'd have a solid direction to follow the evidence.

A knock at his door had him swinging back around. Spotting Kyle standing there, he smiled.

"Don't just loiter in the doorway, Ace. You're making the place look untidy."

Laughing, Kyle stepped into the room while showing Gray the finger.

"How's it going, old man?"

"I swear running through quicksand would be easier than trying to solve this case. What's the link I'm missing, Kyle?

What is it about this accelerant pattern that is so unusual, yet strangely familiar? I know it's something that I've seen before, I just can't seem to figure out where."

"I'm about to go see Matthews. Why don't you give yourself a break and come with me? Maybe stepping away from it will give you clearer vision. Sometimes we go over the stuff so often we miss what's hiding in plain sight."

Nodding, Gray got to his feet. "Yeah, you're probably right. Let me grab my jacket and we can hit the road." Shrugging his coat on, he continued, "Want to use my vehicle?"

"Sure, why not?"

Keeping conversation light on the way to the hospital, they talked about inconsequential things, staying away from the topic of the case.

"So, old man, fess up. How's the dating going?"

Gray glanced at Kyle briefly before returning his eyes back to the road.

"What's got you so interested in my love life, Ace?"

"Curiosity. You're normally the love 'em and leave 'em type, but this lady's been in the picture for longer than any other. I'm curious to know what's so special about this one."

Gray took a moment before answering, "I don't know what it is about her. I just know I've never felt the way I do when I'm around her with anyone else. She's sweet and feisty, and when she looks at you, it feels like she sees you. Really sees *you*, you know?"

This time it was Kyle's turn to be silent for a moment. "Nope, I can't honestly say I do know, bud." Gray thought he detected a note of what sounded like longing in the man's voice.

"I don't know, Ace. There's something special about her. I never thought I'd say these words, but for the first time, ever, I want to see where this can go."

Pulling into the parking lot at the hospital, Gray killed the engine. Neither moved at first, reluctant to get out and face the realities of their job. Finally, Kyle turned to Gray.

"Best of luck, bud. I hope it works out for you."

Climbing out, Kyle rounded the front of the vehicle and waited for Gray to join him. Making their way through the front doors, they said nothing further as they headed for their colleague's room with heavy hearts.

***

Standing back to get a better look at the overall effect she was creating, Kitty stretched tired muscles. She'd been bent over, icing for what seemed like forever. Hearing a sound behind her, she turned to see Jazz coming into the kitchen.

"So, what do you think?"

"Looking good. You've really nailed that intricate piece. Just like I said you would."

Laughing at Jazz, Kitty replied, "Yes, you did, didn't you? I hear the 'I told you so' in there."

With an innocent look on her elfin face, she replied, "Me? Never!" before laughing along with Kitty. "Listen, before I forget why I came in, Lee's in the store asking for you. But, be warned, Archie is lurking. He's in to get his daily fix."

Pulling a face of her own, Kitty groaned. "Damn. Okay, I'll be there in a minute. I just need to wash my hands."

"Sure thing. I'll let Lee know."

Peeking around the corner, Kitty tried to see if there was any way to sneak past Archie. Seeing his attention directed away from the doorway she stepped into the storefront to gesture Lee into the kitchen. Just as she thought she'd get away with it, Archie turned and spotted her.

"Hi, Kitty. Hi. You're looking beautiful today." His whole face lit up as his eyes greedily took her in.

"Oh, hey, Archie. How are you?" She tried to signal Lee past her so she could make good an escape back to the kitchen as soon as possible without Archie noticing. Finally, she got the hint. Nodding, she slipped past Kitty.

"Um, Kitty…... Er, I was – um, was wondering. Would you have coffee with me?" His eagerness was palpable. Looking at him, she realised how unfair she was being to him. By constantly putting him off with a casual "maybe another time" each time he asked, she was giving him false hope. It was best to rip the plaster off and just tell him no.

Turning to Lee standing behind her, Kitty spoke softly. "Just give me a sec. I need to take care of this quickly."

Nodding, but saying nothing, Lee acknowledged her.

"Archie, let's have a chat over here," she said, indicating a corner away from all the movement and noise. A corner where she could let him down easy and no one would hear it. "Archie, I don't know how to say this without hurting your feelings, so I'm just going to say it." As gently as she could, Kitty continued. "I've met someone recently, and we've really hit it off. Since we're only just getting to know each other, I don't think he'll like it if I went out for coffee with you. I'm really sorry, Archie."

An unpleasant look crossed his face before his features settled into a blank look. As brief as the look had been, it made Kitty uncomfortable. She wasn't quite sure what the look was, but she didn't think it was anything good.

"I don't – I don't think that's – that's…..." he stammered, his facing going red. Taking a breath, he tried again. "I don't think that's very nice of you, Kitty," he lisped. His tone short, she realised he was upset. Very upset.

"Archie, I really am sorry. I never meant to hurt your feelings."

"Well, I – it…..... It wasn't very nice to make me think that you would someday. And – and – and now, you say you can't because of someone else. That's…..... that's not very nice. I thought you were a nice person, but it – it, ah…..... It seems I was wrong."

Marching to the door, he gave her one last disgruntled look and stormed out of the shop.

Having turned to see what the ruckus was about, Jazz saw Archie storm out. "Hey Archie, your cupcake," she called after him, holding the packaged cupcake up. He gave no response as he continued to rush away.

Sighing, Kitty turned towards the kitchen and spotted Lee standing in the doorway, where she'd left her to speak to Archie. Reaching her friend, she said, "Come then. I need coffee now."

The other woman looked quizzically at her but didn't give voice to her thoughts.

"I can hear the questions from over here. Ask what you want to ask." Handing Lee a mug, Kitty went into her office off the kitchen and settled in her chair.

Taking a seat opposite Kitty, Lee eventually asked, "What on earth was all that about? Archie seemed mighty pissed about something."

Sighing once more, Kitty replied, "He asked me to have coffee with him again. I've been putting him off for ages, but I figured today I would grow a backbone and finally tell him no. I don't want to lead him on. Every time I tell him 'maybe next time', it gives him hope that it'll happen when it won't. I have no intention of ever going for coffee with him. And it wasn't fair to keep letting him think otherwise."

"Ahh," was all Lee said before taking a sip of her coffee. The long look Lee gave her had Kitty almost squirming in her seat.

"Urgh, don't look at me like that. I already feel bad."

"Babe, Morgs and I have been warning you about this for the longest time. You had to know it was coming," Lee finally replied.

"Yeah, I knew it. It *has* been coming for a long time. I should never have left it this long. And that only makes me feel worse."

Waving a hand, Lee swallowed a mouthful of coffee before saying, "It's done. No good beating yourself up about it now. Give him time; he'll get over it. In the meantime, tell me about you. How are you doing? What have you been up to? And most importantly, how did the date go the other night?"

Putting the ugly scene with Archie out of her mind, Kitty grinned. "Oh my god, it was such a fabulous evening. Gray treated me to dinner and dancing. Let me just tell you, that man can move. Girl, if he dances like that, I'd like to know what else he can do that well."

"A man that dances! You got lucky, babes. That's a rare breed."

"Tell me about it."

"You really like him, don't you?" Lee asked, giving Kitty another of those penetrating looks.

"I really do, Lee. He's confident and comfortable in his own skin. That's so refreshing and such a turn on."

Jazz appeared at the office door. "Sorry to interrupt the girl time, but the hottie fire investigator is out front asking for you. And oh my god, he's got another hot guy with him."

"I'll be right there. Thanks, Jazz."

"Oh no, ma'am. It is I who should be thanking you for all this amazing eye-candy you appear to be attracting into the store these days."

Tossing an eraser at Jazz, Kitty laughed at the younger woman.

"If you don't mind letting me out, I'll zip out the back

here. I need to get going anyway. It's time to head back to the office." Lee stood.

"Sure thing, babes. Thanks for the visit. I'll chat to you later."

<hr>

How could she? All we ever wanted was for her to be happy, to love us. We've done everything for her, and this is how she repays us! Tears of anger gathered in their eyes. Rocking back and forth, they continued to express their anger, whispering to themselves. For hours they simply rocked, mumbling and plotting. She needed to be punished. What would hurt her? Hurt her like she'd hurt them? She must be made to feel their pain. And as the thought came to them, their eyes shone with malicious joy. Yes! They knew exactly what needed to be done.

Candlelight softened the room. Her iPod played softly in the background. The warm water rippled over her as she moved her foot back and forth. It had been a busy day. Tired and feeling the strain of having spent the day bent over, Kitty had decided a warm, scented bath was just the thing to make her feel better.

Relaxing against the back of the bath, her thoughts turned again to Gray. Thoughts of him had been on her mind since he'd popped in. He'd looked tired, but more than that, he'd looked down. Everything in her had wanted to offer him comfort. But she hadn't wanted to make him uncomfortable in front of his friend.

The thought not even cold yet, her cell phone rang, and she saw his number on the screen. Smiling, she answered, "Hi Gray."

"Hi yourself." She could hear a smile in his voice. "Are you busy this evening?"

"Not particularly. I don't have any plans. I figured a quiet night in was the ticket. You?"

"Well, that depends."

"On what?" she asked, biting her lip.

"On you," he replied.

"Oh. How so? What did you have in mind?" His soft laugh made everything girly in her sit up and take notice.

"You up for company? I haven't eaten yet, and since I don't want to eat alone, thought maybe I could pick up some take-out for us... and head over to your place for that quiet evening in. I'd really like to see you again. You haven't eaten yet, have you?"

That, just that, made Kitty feel her heart squeeze. She couldn't remember when last a man had made her feel like that. If ever. And she liked it. She liked it a lot.

"No, I haven't eaten. I decided a long soak in the bath with a glass of wine was the first order of business this evening. But I could definitely eat now."

"Excellent. Do you eat sushi?"

"Hmm, yes. I love sushi."

"I'll grab some and head on over then, if that's okay with you?"

"That'd be great."

"Anything in particular you like? Anything I need to stay away from?"

"Other than eel and tuna, I'm game for pretty much anything else."

"Gotcha, consider it done. See you shortly."

"I'll see you in a bit then."

"Yeah, later," he replied in that sinful voice of his.

Hurrying out of the bath, Kitty dashed around getting herself dressed and making sure the apartment was company ready. Humming to herself, she got out plates and soy sauce ramekins, put a bottle of white wine in the fridge to cool, and took out clean glasses.

Just as she was putting the finishing touches to the dining table, the downstairs buzzer sounded. Running her hands nervously over her hair one last time, she went to get the door.

Opening it, she took a moment to absorb the sight of Gray standing on her threshold. Her mouth watered, and it most definitely wasn't the sushi causing it. He was casually dressed in well-worn jeans and a T-shirt that lovingly hugged every chiselled muscle underneath. Clearly, he was no slouch when it came to staying fit.

"Hi again." He smiled.

"Hi." Stepping aside so he could enter, she smiled up at him. "Come on in. Welcome to my home." Leading the way, she headed for the kitchen.

"Thank you. I come bearing food. Where would you like me to put it?"

"In the kitchen, but I thought we could eat at the table in the dining room, if that's okay with you?"

"Sure, that sounds perfect. Lead the way."

D inner over and dishes done, Kitty led Gray into the living room.

"Have a seat. Can I get you some more wine before I sit?"

Sitting, he shook his head. "I'm driving, so no more for me."

"I have an early start, so I should probably switch to something else too. How about some coffee?"

"Sounds great, thanks," he replied.

By the time she'd made coffee, Gray had found her iPod and was searching her playlists. Choosing a song, he returned the iPod to its docking station, and music began to play softly.

"I see you're a Nickelback fan," he said as he took the tray from her.

"Yep, nothing like Nickelback cranked up good and loud to keep you company on the early morning drive in to work. When most everyone else is still snuggled down in their beds and I'd far rather be there too."

With a laugh, he returned to his spot on the sofa. "I would never have pictured you as a rock chick, but I think it's pretty hot."

Sitting facing him on the sofa with her knee drawn up on the cushion, she blushed, not knowing how to respond.

Laughing again, he teased, "You have to be the only woman I know who blushes. And you even manage to make that look graceful." His smile fading, Gray leaned forward and wrapped his hands around her upper arms, gently tugging her over until she was sitting in his lap.

At first, Kitty was unsure of herself. Sitting in Gray's lap was a new experience for her. She'd never felt comfortable doing it; she always worried she was too heavy. But he seemed oblivious to her inner turmoil. Clearly it wasn't an issue for him, so she decided to just go with it.

They talked for a while, about this and that, getting to know each other a bit better. Seeing Gray was quite at ease with their situation, Kitty finally settled into him and was feeling a sense of peace she hadn't felt since the fires in the area had started. As he ran his hand up and down her arm idly, she felt him begin to relax beneath her.

"Tell me about your day," Kitty requested.

"Well, there've been two highs in my day. Kyle and I popped in to see Matthews – that's where we'd come from when I popped in at the bakery. He's pulled through, against all odds, and has now been transferred from ICU to High Care." Pausing, he leaned his forehead against hers, one of his hands going to the back of her neck, holding her to him.

"That is good news. I'm glad to hear he's doing okay,

Gray. And the second?" She bit her lip as she waited for his response.

She watched as he followed the movement with his eyes, saw them darkened with desire. It kindled an answering burn within her. Shifting position, Kitty straddled Gray.

"Knowing I'd get to see you again tonight." Pausing, he looked into her eyes, before he continued, "Fair warning Kitty, I'm going to kiss you again. I can't help myself. When you do that biting thing? It drives me nuts."

Using the hand he'd wrapped around the back of her neck, he slowly drew her in.

With a sigh, she softened and relaxed into him, wrapping her arms around his neck. He deepened the kiss as she felt him harden beneath her. Ever so slowly, he slid his hands under her T-shirt. Running his hands gently up and down her back, she marvelled at how different his skin felt from her own. She was soft in contrast to the hard of his.

Kitty arched her back into his palms, loving the feel of his calloused hands against her skin. She tugged on his shirt, wanting to feel him under her hands, wanting no barrier. Reaching behind him, between his shoulder blades, he pulled the material over his head and tossed it aside, seeming to want no barrier either. Placing her hands back on his chest, Gray slid his hands back under her T-shirt and undid the clasp of her bra.

He was driving her slowly out of her mind. She lifted her arms when he pulled her shirt up so he could remove it. But before she could put her hands back on him, he leaned her back far enough to capture a plump, tightly furled nipple between his teeth. As he clamped down, firmly but gently, Kitty was sure she was going to come out of her skin. She was so wet for him already she was surprised he couldn't smell her arousal. She *ached* for him. Moaning low in her throat, she held on to him, wrapping her hands around the beautifully defined muscles of his arms.

***

*S*tanding on the sidewalk, staring up at her window, they ranted to themselves. Her betrayal cut deep. That should be them up there. Not that upstart fire investigator. Who does he think he is? He's done nothing but cause them anguish. She was theirs until he'd come along and interfered, damn it! They had hoped it wouldn't come to this, but it seemed there was no other option now.

***

He felt her moan all the way through him. Already so hard for her, he thought he'd come out of his skin. He had to get inside her. Inside her sweet, gentle goodness he was getting to know. But he was also coming to realise under all that there was a bit of a wild child. He couldn't wait to coax her out to come and play.

Reaching between them, he slid the zip of her jeans down and pushed his hands into the back of her pants. When his fingers encountered all that glorious flesh exposed by her thong, he couldn't hold back a moan of his own.

Gray murmured huskily against her lips, "God, Kitty, I need you so badly I can almost taste it." He kneaded the firm globes beneath his hands.

At his words, Kitty ran her tongue over her bottom lip, her eyes liquid pools of need. Gray followed the little pink tip's progress and felt himself harden even more, almost painfully. What was it about this woman that pushed all his buttons? He'd seen his share of beautiful women. Even had his fair share. But there was just something special about Katherine Spence that got him all wound up.

Laying her out on the couch, he stretched out beside her, partially lying on the cushions so as not to crush her with his weight. Sliding his hands out of the back of her jeans, he slid one hand down the front of them and paused as his hand lay over her mound.

"Kitty, be very sure this is something you want. I know we've only known each other a short while, but if this progresses to full-blown sex, there's no going back. This is not a quick fuck for me. If we do this, I'll want more. You need to be sure this is something you want too."

Her only reply was to reach up and softly place her lips on his. When she ran the tip of her tongue lightly over his bottom lip, he slid a finger down and over her clit, mimicking the movement. Her hips shifted restlessly beneath his touch.

Rubbing over the tight bundle of nerves, he growled, "I have to have you, baby. I want to taste you so bad."

Kitty pushed gently on his chest as she worked herself out from under him. Rising gracefully, she led him down the hall into her bedroom.

Kitty closed the door behind them. Settling his palms against the closed door on either side of her head, he leaned in to kiss her. Before she could catch her breath, he picked her up and carried her over to the bed. He lowered her gently before he stepped back to discard the rest of his clothing.

Kitty biting her lip as he watched her watching his every move made him all kinds of hot.

"Honey, if you keep biting on your lip like that, I can't be held responsible for what I do. It's incredibly sexy. Drives me crazy, every damn time."

She gave him a slow smile and murmured, "What's taking so long?"

"Oh, it's like that, is it?" he drawled. Kitty just bit her lip in reply.

The rest of his clothes came off in a rush, and she barely had time to admire the beauty of him in all his ripped, naked glory. Climbing onto the bed, he reached for her.

"You're wearing way too much clothing, baby. Let's get you out of them, shall we?" His husky murmur in her ear sent shivers of anticipation down her spine.

As Kitty wriggled out of her pants and thong, she had a moment's doubt. She was curvy. Not all cut like some of the woman she saw at the gym on the days she actually had the time and energy to go. Would he be put off that she was soft and had curves, not cut and buff like gym bunnies? As if he sensed her thoughts, Gray ran a hand down her sides and around to the curve of her ass, humming low in his chest.

"Gorgeous. There's nothing more beautiful than a woman that looks like a woman should. Curves for a man to hold on to." His breath feathered over a nipple. The soft exhalation of air caused the tight little pebble to tighten more, pouting for attention. And he seemed only too happy to oblige. Nipping gently, he ran a soothing tongue over the bud in his mouth. His cheeks hollowed as he sucked her in deeper.

With a soft cry, she arched into him, silently begging for more. Gray let the tightened bud slip out of his mouth, before he repeated the action on the other one. Working his way down her body, taking his time, he dropped gentle kisses on her skin until he reached the core of her femininity. Using his thumbs, he parted her swollen lips and groaned.

"So wet. Damn woman, you're killing me here. I'm trying to make this good for you, but when I see you so ready for me..."

She was wet and swollen, so aroused she was ready to climb out of her skin.

He ran his finger over her clit, and she arched off the bed, moaning softly. Kitty pushed her fingers into his hair to anchor herself against the myriad emotions. Using his tongue, he continued to lavish attention on her clit. He added a finger to her tight channel, rubbing against the sweet spot. Kitty writhed beneath him, her core slick with her desire.

As he inserting another finger, Gray curved them to hit the sweet spot again.

"You're so tight. God, it's going to feel so good, but I don't want to hurt you, baby."

"Gray," she whimpered.

"Shh, honey, I'll take care of you."

Slowly working his fingers in and out while turning his attention back to her clit, he pushed her higher. As she drew closer and closer to the edge, Kitty felt her body tighten. She was primed and ready to explode. And then she fell into the freefall of sensation. Unable to hold it back, she cried out as she climaxed, her core gripped his fingers as if they never wanted to let him go.

Pressing butterfly kisses to the inside of her thigh, he grinned. "Ready to do it again?"

"I've got a better idea," she purred.

"Oh yes?" He arched a brow.

She gave him a wicked smile, patting the bed beside her. "Come on up here, and I'll show you."

Moving up the bed and rolling to his back, he quipped, "I'm all yours, baby."

With a lick of her lips, she leaned forward and ran her tongue around the head of his shaft. She worked her way up and down that rock-hard cock, licked and nibbled. Kitty looked up at him and, holding his gaze, she slowly took him into the warm, wet cavern of her mouth. There was no missing the flare of heat that lit his eyes. Fisting the base in one hand and taking his balls in the other, she fucked him with her mouth until he thought he'd go out of his mind.

"Kitty, honey, stop. I don't want it to end like this." He groaned. "I want to be inside you when it happens."

Ever so slowly, she crawled up his body to straddle him. Reaching into her nightstand drawer, she pulled a condom out. With a silent prayer it hadn't expired, she ripped the foil and in one smooth motion, unrolled it down his very impressive length before lifting herself. She wrapped her hand around him, guiding him to her entrance. Her gaze to his once again, she lowered herself onto him, loving the burn she felt as he stretched her. Tossing her head as she took all of him, they moan simultaneously.

"God, you're so tight. I'm not going to last," he gasped.

With a wicked smile, holding nothing back, Kitty rode him until they both found their release. As Kitty's orgasm crashed over her, she dug her nails into Gray's chest as if to anchor herself, lost in a sea of sensation. She collapsed onto his heaving chest, trying to control her breathing.

Kitty eventually became aware of Gray stroking his hands gently up and down her back. Shifting so her chin rested on the back of her hand that lay on the middle of his chest, she looked down at him. With a smile, he brought a hand around to gently run his knuckles down her cheek.

"I need to use the bathroom a second, honey."

Kitty rolled off onto the bed and stretched luxuriously as Gray got up. Padding towards the bathroom, he spoke over his shoulder.

"I'll be right back. Keep a spot warm for me."

A very contented "Hmm" was all he got in reply.

Returning to the bed, he pulled Kitty into his arms. Smothering a huge yawn, she snuggled into his embrace and smiled up at him, absently rubbing a hand over his pecs.

"You look beat. It seems I've worn you out."

Laughing in response, Kitty nodded.

"Yep, so you have."

Placing a gentle kiss on her forehead, he watched her close her eyes.

"Get some rest then. Night, honey."

"Night, Gray." She slipped into sleep with a soft smile on her face.

K itty gently rubbing a soft hand over his chest was soothing Gray into a calm lull. As his mind emptied of any thoughts but of her, he held her a little closer. Placing a gentle kiss on Kitty's forehead, he pulled back to look at her. Watching as she closed her eyes and drifted off to sleep, he felt a sense of calm settle over him, a calm he hadn't felt in weeks.

That was when he knew he was in trouble. In that moment, holding a warm and soft Kitty in his arms, he *knew* there was nowhere on earth he'd rather be. He was exactly where he was meant to be.

He realised this feeling that had been circling round the edge of his thoughts, the one he couldn't put a name to, was what Kitty made him feel. He suspected it was love, but Gray wasn't sure he was ready to face it, name it, claim it. For the moment, he just wanted to enjoy this beautiful woman's company and get to know her. Let her get to know him. See where it went.

Leaning over to the side, he turned the lamp on the bedside table off, plunging the room into darkness. Pulling Kitty back into his embrace, he folded a hand behind his head and followed her into sleep. The first easy sleep since the arsonist had started playing cat and mouse games.

Their rage knew no bounds now as they watched the lights go out in her apartment. They were beyond rage. Ungrateful whore! They'd waited for her to realise she was theirs. They'd been patient. Courted her in their own way, the only way they knew how. Put themselves in danger for her. And this was the thanks they got? They couldn't believe their beloved was just like every other woman. Nothing but a common whore!

Sobbing out their hurt and rage, they threw things around the room. Taking a red marker, they began to draw crosses over her face. Methodically, they worked their way around the room. Over the years, they'd lovingly collected thousands of photos. But now, that love was gone. She'd killed it. Systematically, they worked to destroy all the photos, just as she'd destroyed their love for her. She would have to pay, and they knew exactly what needed to be done. They would make her very sorry she'd given the love that was their due to another.

CHAPTER 8

G ray rooted blindly around the pedestal next to the bed for his ringing phone. Squinting against the glare of the screen, he noted Kyle's number on its display.

"This better be good, Ace. What the hell time is it anyway?"

"Hey, Gray, sorry to wake you, man. It's almost a quarter to two. Are you bunked down somewhere here at the station?" Kyle queried.

"No, I didn't sleep at the station last night. I'll meet you there. What's the address?"

Kyle's momentary silence had the tiny hairs on the back of his neck rising. "I'm sorry, bud, I hate to be the one to tell you, but it's that fancy bakery place that belongs to your new girlfriend."

"Are you sure? No, don't bother answering that. Of course you're sure. Jesus." Running a hand over his face he continued, "Give me a bit of time. I'll meet you there."

He felt a heavy weight settle over him as he hung up. Sighing, he rolled to his back and beat his head against his pillow once as he tried to figure out how to tell her. Thankfully, his gear was still in his truck from the day before so he could head straight out to the scene.

Reaching out, he turned the side lamp on before rolling onto his side. He tucked himself in behind Kitty's sleeping form. He was glad she'd slept through the call. Knowing he was about to devastate her, he wished he could be anywhere else right now, doing anything other than having to wake her. Shaking her gently, he braced himself.

"Hmmmph," came the very disgruntled objection.

"Kitty, I need you to wake up, baby. I need to talk to you."

"'Sa time?"

Smiling despite being about to crush her, he placed soft kisses on her temple. Apparently, Kitty didn't do well being woken up.

"Just a little before two."

Rolling towards Gray, she opened a squinty eye.

"In the morning?"

His woman definitely didn't seem to do mornings. Something he best make a mental note of for future reference. But right now, there was a more pressing matter he needed to attend to.

"Are you with me, honey? I need you to focus on what I'm about to tell you."

Something in his tone must have penetrated the sleep fog in her brain. She rolled all the way over, facing him, both eyes now open.

"Baby, I don't know how to tell you this, but I have some bad news."

"Just say it, Gray."

Taking a deep breath, he said, "My guys are responding to a call out. I need to... ah shit, Kitty, I'm sorry baby. The call is for Decadence. They're responding to a fire at Decadence. I'm so sorry, baby."

Gray watched as all the colour leached out of Kitty's face. As crappy as he felt in that moment, having to be the one to tell her, he could only imagine what she was feeling right then. She had put her heart and soul into building Decadence up, and to have someone maliciously burn that hard work to the ground had to hurt.

"What? *What*? Decadence is burning? Are you sure?" If it wasn't so sad, Gray would have laughed as Kitty repeated his words to Kyle minutes earlier. "Of course you are. Oh God."

Gray watched as she drew her knees up to her chest, a purely instinctive measure of protection against further hurts. Knowing there was nothing he could do or say to make her feel better, he vowed to find the person responsible and get justice for her. He would find them, he silently vowed to Kitty. Getting out of bed, he urged her to do the same.

"Come on, honey. We need to get going."

Without another word, she suddenly dashed out of the bed and started getting dressed. Gray followed suit, pulling on his own clothes. Watching her get dressed, he was worried by the grey hue of her skin.

She almost looked ill. He could see the emotional pain she was suffering in her eyes, almost as if it had been a physical blow. He went to her and drew her into his arms, tucking her head under his chin and resting it on top of her head; he rubbed soothing strokes up and down her back.

"I know this is a huge blow to you, baby, but I need to get going. I don't like the idea of leaving you here alone. Do you want to go with me?"

He felt her nod of assent. Putting a comforting arm around her, he steered her out of the room into the lounge so he could find his T-shirt. Allowing him to guide her, Kitty walked beside him. When they reached the parking area of her complex, he helped her into the car before circling around to climb in beside her. They drove to Decadence in grim silence, Gray holding her hand the whole way.

K itty could feel Gray's eyes on her constantly. But she was so caught up in her own misery she wasn't able to offer him assurances she'd be okay. Decadence had been her life. She'd invested more than just money into her business. Her heart and soul had gone into making it all that it had been. Now it was gone. All of it.

No, not Decadence. Decadence was gone. Nothing more than ash and lost dreams. What was she supposed to do now?

She felt raw. Like she was about to come out of her skin. And she didn't know how to deal with how she was feeling. So how could she tell Gray she was okay when she really wasn't?

Instead, Kitty held her silence, staring out at the passing darkness. Sitting still, her body clenched, as if she could hold herself together by pure will alone. If she moved too quickly, she might just shatter into a million pieces. Pieces that would never be found again, so when she put herself back together, she'd be incomplete.

Closing her eyes against the pain, Kitty's mind flooded with memories. Of the early years. The months leading up to the opening. She'd worked herself to the bone to make sure all would go off without a hitch. She remembered the excitement and nervousness.

Opening day had been the culmination of hard work and dreams fulfilled. Everything she wanted and more. And now, now it was all gone. Nothing left to show how much of herself she'd invested into making Decadence a reality.

Kitty wanted nothing more than to scream out her pain. To break things, throw things. Rail at the fates. Why had they done this to her? *Who* had done this to her? She didn't understand how she found herself here. So how could she reassure Gray she was fine? She wasn't.

———

Gray kept glancing over at Kitty. She was deathly pale and hadn't said a word since before they'd left the apartment. He reached out to take her hand, squeezing gently to let her know he was there for her. Holding on to his hand, she sat, unmoving, until they reached Decadence.

Pulling up near to the crime tape, he parked and turned the truck off. Turning to her, Gray ran his fingers down her face, coming to rest under her chin. With gentle but firm pressure, he turned her face so he could look into her eyes.

"Kitty, I need to go speak to my guys. Will you be okay waiting here? Or would you rather go with me?" She just shook her head and reached for the door handle. "Sit tight. I'll come around." He got out of the cab and came around to open the door for her.

To the untrained eye, chaos reigned, but in truth it was a well-rehearsed choreography. Each member of the team knew where they needed to be and what they needed to be doing. Knowing just where to find him, Gray made his way directly to command central. Gray was glad to spot Jeff Erickson manning the post. The fire scene couldn't be in better hands.

. . .

"Hi, Jeff." Putting a hand out to shake the older man's, he then turned to Kitty, saying, "This is Katherine Spence. She's the owner to the bakery." Gray gestured to the burning building. "Kitty, this is Jeffrey Erickson."

"Ms Spence, it's nice to meet you." The elder gentleman smiled kindly at her. "I'm just sorry it has to be under these conditions."

Trying valiantly to pull herself together, Kitty stuck her hand out, replying, "It's nice to meet you too, Mr Erickson."

"Jeff, what can you tell me?" Gray asked.

"Stevens, Collins, and Links are in there now. I'll know more when they come out, but they've found the point of origin. And it seems our firebug left something behind this time. Stevens says it's somewhat mangled due to the fire, but if anyone can work magic, it's you. I'm sure you'll get something useful out of it."

"It's about time we caught a break. I'm taking him down this time."

"Sir, we're coming out. Search and rescue done, all clear. Looks like James has scored this time. Hopefully, we can nail this bastard now." Kyle's voice sounded over Jeff's radio.

"Copy that, Stevens," Jeff responded.

Turning to watch, they saw the three men clear the doorway and head towards where they were standing. Just as they reached them, a shower of sparks lit up the night sky as the building finally collapsed in on herself.

That moment was like a red-hot poker to the chest. Suddenly, Kitty felt as if she couldn't catch a breath. Like an enormous weight had settled on her chest and it wouldn't allow her to breathe. Fanciful maybe, but it felt as if the last of her dreams had collapsed right along with her building. In the far reaches of her mind, she knew it wasn't the truth. She could start over, that this wasn't the end of it. But in that moment, that's exactly how it felt. Five years of blood, sweat, and tears had just collapsed in a spectacular shower of sparks. Gone.

So focused on the scene unfolding before her, she didn't even feel the tears that streamed down her face. Only when Gray reached out and wiped at them did she notice. She couldn't see past her tears, but she felt his strength, his gentle touch. Turning to him, she burrowed into his warmth as he enfolded her in his arms. A single sob escaped.

"It's okay, honey. I'm here. Give it to me," he whispered.

Unable to help herself, she pressed closer yet, giving in to all the misery and heartache swirling in a painful mix within her. Her body shook with the intensity of the emotions as they poured out. For a long time, they simply stood like that as all movement ebbed and flowed around them. The gentle hand Gray continued to rub up and down her back soothed, giving comfort. Eventually, all the emotion spent, she stood unmoving in his embrace and absorbed the quiet strength that he offered.

Standing at the scene of a fire was always exhilarating but especially so when it was one of their own. They'd pulled all the stops out for this one, making sure nothing would remain standing. They wanted her to feel the same pain that twisted them up inside. She'd hurt them deeply, and they wanted her to know just how much. Now she did. Looking over at where she stood, their face contorted with fury. Whore! Look at you, allowing him to paw at you in public. Now you know what it feels like to lose everything you hold dear. Now you know what that tearing pain feels like as you watch your dreams go up in smoke. We would have given you everything, anything. We waited for you, patiently. You've taken it all away and now you suffer like we do.

CHAPTER 9

As she listened to the ringing, Kitty braced herself. She knew sharing the news with her mother not only made it real, but Elenore Spence had the skills of a seasoned investigator. She would seek clarity until the situation had been looked at from every angle, then she'd slip into full Mother Mode, set on fixing all hurts. It was her way.

"Hello, darling," Elenore's melodious voice sounded in Kitty's ear.

"Hi Mom," she started to reply, but her voice broke at the end. The comfort and security her mother represented always made it difficult for her to speak to her mother when her world was upside down. It made her more tearful.

"Kitty? What's the matter, baby? Are you all right?" The concern in her mother's voice broke the tenuous hold she had on her emotions, and she couldn't get another word out. To do so would require her to be able to breathe. And right that minute, the enormous pressure was back, compressing her lungs.

Thrusting the phone in an unsuspecting Gray's direction, Kitty bolted. She didn't see the concern creasing his face as he watched her run. She dashed from the room as if the hounds of hell themselves where on her trail, seeking the sanctuary of her bedroom. Desperate to draw a deep breath, almost hyperventilating in her grief, a distant part of her brain noted she needed to calm herself.

Standing in the middle of her bedroom, she wasn't quite sure what to do with herself. Her thoughts were fragmented and frantic. The emotions she'd pushed to the back of her mind while dealing with officials at the fire scene were now making themselves felt. Loss, fear, confusion – they all vied for attention.

A small part of her felt bad for abandoning Gray to deal with her mother, but Kitty should have known it would happen. It always did. She should have waited a bit longer or maybe asked her mother to come over. Phoning her had been a bad idea.

Feeling lost, adrift in her misery, she simply stood there, unmoving. Unsure of how long it had been, Kitty finally sank to her knees, giving vent to the maelstrom that churned within. Harsh sobs rasped her throat and shock sent shudders through her frame as she wrapped her arms tightly around herself.

When, eventually, there were no more tears left to cry, Kitty crawled over to her bed. Sheer exhaustion left her weak and barely able to keep her eyes open. Dragging herself up onto the bed, she burrowed under the exquisite quilt her grandmother had made for her when she was a baby, seeking comfort in the familiar. As tired as she was, sleep eluded her. Thoughts and feelings buzzed around in brain, keeping blissful surrender just out of her grasp.

"**H**ello? Kitty? *Hello?*" The frantic voice on the other side drew his attention, and he realised he had yet to speak.

"Sorry, Mrs Spence. Hi. My name is Grayson James. I'm a friend of Kitty's. She's somewhat upset. There's no easy way to say this, I'm afraid. There was another fire in the Kloofnek area, and this time it was Decadence that burned down this morning. As you can imagine, Kitty's taking it very hard. Much as I'd love to, unfortunately, I am unable to stay here with her, and I don't like the idea of leaving her alone right now."

"Oh my God! Is Kitty okay? I mean physically. What happened? Was she there when it happened?"

"Easy there, Mrs Spence. Physically, she's fine. The fire occurred in the early hours of this morning, so no one was there, thankfully. I took her down as soon as we heard, and we've only just returned. In fact, that's where I need to get back to, which is why I wondered if you could come over and stay with her."

"Yes. Yes, of course. I'm on my way. And Mr James?"

"Yes, ma'am?"

"Thank you for taking care of my daughter. I'm glad she has someone with her. Since I don't recall having met you, I look forward to it. See you shortly."

Gray hung up the phone and went in search of Kitty. He found her curled in a ball, huddled under the blanket on her bed. Pulling her into his arms, he rocked her, running a soothing hand up and down her back. Pressing kisses to her temple, he said, "I'm so sorry this happened to you, baby."

She nodded but didn't reply, just tightened her grip on his neck while resting her head on his shoulder.

"Your mom's on her way over. I'll wait with you until she gets here and then I must go. I wish I could stay, but I need to head over to the site so I can start my investigation. I'm going to nail this bastard if it's the last thing I do."

"Thank you, Gray," Kitty whispered into his neck.

They sat like that until the downstairs buzzer sounded. Setting her down gently on the bed, he went to open up for her mother. Kitty could hear them murmuring in the lounge but couldn't muster up the energy to go out to meet her mom. Eventually, they made their way into the room. Her mother rushed over to her, gathering her in her arms. Gray leaned down to place a sweet kiss on her lips.

"I'll be back as soon as I can."

"Okay. Gray? Just– Be safe, okay?"

Nodding, he turned to leave, letting himself out quietly. Thoughts already shifting to the situation at hand.

There was no end to their treachery. They'd thought that the message was very clear, would warn him away, show her they were serious, but they should have known. If she could betray them once, why wouldn't she do it again? The pain twisted in their gut and madness roiled in their mind. Those two would pay. Just as soon as the time was right, they'd make them pay.

At some point, she must have fallen asleep. Coming awake slowly, Kitty realised she must have slept for quite some time since her bedside lamp was now on and the curtains drawn. It seemed she'd slept the day away.

Jerking upright, she also realised she hadn't let Jazz know. Searching for her cell phone, sure she would find numerous calls from her, she came up emptyhanded. Where the hell was the damn thing? Frantically, she ran into the lounge to look for her handbag, stopping short when she saw her mom and Gray sitting chatting quietly.

"There's my gorgeous girl," her mom said as she rose to hug Kitty.

Leaning her head on her mom's shoulder, she turned to Gray, giving him a small smile.

"Hi," she greeted them both. "Have either of you seen my cell phone? I completely forgot to phone Jazz in all the pandemonium this morning. And now I've slept the rest of the day away. She must be out of her mind with worry by now."

Getting to his feet, he returned her smile before saying, "Don't worry about Jazz. I got her number from your mom and called her on my way out this morning. I told her you'd call as soon as you were able to."

Going over to where he stood, she put her arms around him, hugging him close. "Thank you. I appreciate it."

"No problem. How are you feeling?"

The concern she saw shining in his beautiful eyes was nearly her undoing. Swallowing past the lump in her throat, she replied, "I'll be okay. I'm really sorry I fell apart on you earlier. I'm not normally such a basket case. It's just, I– It was..." She stumbled to a stop. Taking a moment, she gathered herself. "It just, I put so much of myself into Decadence. All I could see was my dream literally going up in smoke. It was, quite possibly, the second most difficult event of my life."

Hugging her tighter to him, he rested his cheek on the top of her head. "I get it. I'm so sorry this happened to you. Kitty, I..." He hesitated, seeming to wrestle with something. Clearing his throat, he stated, "Kitty, this isn't just a social call. And god knows, this isn't an easy conversation I need to have with you. But you're going to have to be told sooner or later."

Kitty stiffened in his embrace before pulling away. Stepping back so she could see his face, she looked at him with eyes gone wide with apprehension. "What is it, Gray?"

"As you know, I was at Decadence today. I went over the site thoroughly, and honey, I'm really sorry to have to tell you. There are definite signs of arson. Decadence was torched on purpose."

What little colour had returned to Kitty's face during the day drained away, leaving her pale with shock. At first, she simply stared at Gray, unable to form a coherent thought. She opened her mouth as if to speak before closing it again, not making a sound.

"Kitty, honey, I'm so sorry."

"But why?" she cried. "Who would hate me that much that they would burn my shop to the ground?"

Guiding her down onto the sofa, he sat beside her, angling his body to included Elenore in the conversation. Taking both her hands in his, he rubbed his thumb in circles over the top of her left hand. Looking into her eyes, glassy with the shock of what she'd just heard, Gray sighed.

"I hate that this has happened to you. You didn't deserve this. But I promise you this. I haven't figured out the who yet, but I will. I've figured out the how though, and that will lead me to the who. I'll figure it out if it's the last thing I do."

"How?" Kitty whispered, her eyes now swimming with tears.

"An arsonist's modus operandi is as unique as a fingerprint. If this is someone who has done this before and they've been caught, we'll have them on record. If not, it'll help me narrow the suspect pool. One way or another, I'll find them."

"What do you mean, Gray?" Elenore asked.

"Well, arsonists tend to be creatures of habit. When it comes to setting the fires, they have a ritual, if you will. They tend to use the same accelerant to start the fire. There's usually a pattern as to how the accelerant is set out, and how quickly they want the fire to burn. How difficult they want to make it to put the blaze out, and so forth. When they find a method that works for them, it's very seldom that that they'll deviate from it. And then, arson is a psychological illness. Once they've had a taste of it, they'll want to do it again."

"Oh, I see. Yes, that makes sense."

"What did you find out today?" Kitty asked.

"Quite a bit actually. There's just something niggling at me. It's like I've seen or heard of this guy before. But for the life of me, I can't seem to put my finger on it. I just wanted to check in, see how you're doing before I head into the office to carry on."

Blushing, she glanced over at her mom. Her mom gave her the "he's a keeper" wink but said nothing.

"Oh. I'm okay, I guess. Well, I will be. It's so much to take in. I just need to work through it. I'm feeling a bit overwhelmed; not sure where to start putting things back to normal. I can't believe someone did this to me intentionally," she replied.

"I know you will, honey. You're strong. That's one of the many things I admire about you."

"I certainly didn't behave like it today. I completely unravelled." She grimaced, embarrassment staining her cheeks.

"Cut yourself some slack, honey. That was a major shock to the system." Gray's voice held a wealth of feeling. A world of unspoken words. Sighing, he continued, "I need to be going, but I'll call you later, okay?"

"I'd like that." She smiled shyly.

He leaned forward to place the gentlest of kisses on her forehead. Getting to his feet, Gray turned to Kitty's mother. "Mrs Spence, it's been a pleasure. I'm just sorry we couldn't meet under better circumstances."

"Darling, the pleasure was all mine," Elenore replied mysteriously.

"Walk me out?" He turned to Kitty, holding out a hand.

Placing her hand in his, she got to her feet. "I'll be right back, Mom," she said, speaking over her shoulder as she walked with him to the front door.

Turning to take her into his arms, Gray said, "Kitty, I don't want to scare you. You've had enough of a crappy day as it is, but I've got a really uncomfortable feeling about this one. Will you do me a favour and stay indoors this evening? Please?"

Swallowing, she nodded. "Okay. I'll ask Mom to stay for supper. We can make dinner together and catch something on the box."

"Thank you, honey. I feel better knowing you'll stay here and that you won't be alone. We'll talk later."

Pulling her in closer, he laid his lips on hers. Sliding his tongue along her bottom lip, he silently asked entry. Opening to him, she let herself sink into the kiss, pushing everything else from her mind. Finally, with regret, he pulled back. "I have to go."

Kitty opened the door for him. "Bye, Gray. I'll talk to you later."

"Yep. Later, babe." Gray waved as he headed for the stairs.

Gray's plans to start combing through the evidence gathered at Decadence were interrupted as he walked into the fire station. Standing talking to a colleague, the station commander called him over when he spotted him.

"Gray, you got a minute?"

"Sure, Chief. What's on your mind?"

"Come on up to my office. I wanted to chat to you about the Kloofnek fires, son."

Excusing himself, Chief Mattison led the way to the stairs.

"Grab a cup of coffee, if you want, and meet me in my office," Mattison said as they reached the landing.

"Yes, sir. Can I get you anything while I'm busy?"

"My usual, thanks." The other man smiled his appreciation as he entered his office.

Carrying the two mugs of steaming coffee, Gray entered the chief's domain. Nodding his thanks, Mattison indicated for Gray to take a seat.

"We've not had a chance to talk about the Kloofnek case in the last few days. Any progress you can report?"

"Nothing further since our last meeting, sir. I've processed the scene of yesterday morning's fire, and I was just on my way to start analysing the evidence I found this morning. We got lucky for the first time since the fires started. The perp left some evidence behind this time. I just need to see if it can be salvaged. and if there's anything useful to extract from it. I'm hoping to have something more positive to report back to you soon, Chief."

"Good, good. Well then, I won't keep you. The higher ups are getting a little nervous about this one since it's so close to our national elections. I don't need to tell you the pressure's on."

"No, sir. I'm fully aware. And I'm working flat-out. I'll get it solved."

"I know you will. You're the best damn investigator I've had the pleasure of working with. I just need you to work your magic as quickly as possible."

"Yes, sir. I'm on it."

"Let me know what you find."

"Yes, sir." Gray knew he was being politely dismissed. Gathering up the empty mugs, he stood. "I'll get to it then."

Nodding, Chief Mattison said no more.

B agging samples to send to the lab, Gray eyed the desk phone sourly as it rang across the room. He hated being interrupted when he was processing evidence. He always worried the distraction would cause him to miss something. Putting the bag in his hand down on the table where he stood, the phone stopped ringing. *"If it's important, they can phone back,"* he muttered to himself.

No sooner had he finished labelling the sample bag he was busy with than the phone started ringing again. *Well, I guess it's important then.* Snorting to himself at his own lame joke, he made his way over to the phone.

"James."

"Saddle up, James. They're calling all hands on-deck. You're going to need your gear," he heard Kyle say.

"On my way." Knowing there'd be time for questions later, he ran to his locker to grab the firefighting gear he stored there but so seldom needed anymore. Although he was no longer on active duty, he was a volunteer firefighter now. It wasn't unusual to get called on to help out when the summer fires burned all over the Cape Peninsula, and even further than that, when there weren't enough full-time firemen.

Sliding down the pole, he took in the group of men gathering just outside. Chief Mattison was clearly waiting for the last of his men to assemble before he spoke.

"All right, settle down." The chatter quietened down as everyone turned their attention to the station commander. He continued, "As you are aware, the fire that started at Silver Mine Reserve is steadily spreading. Despite our best efforts, the wind and weather have been making things very difficult. Unfortunately, the prevailing winds have been picking up steadily all day. They're calling all local hands in, as well as having put out a call for assistance from the Eastern Cape and Orange Free State provinces. So, suit up ladies and gents, we're going in."

Kyle came over to where Gray stood. "You got everything you need, bud?"

"Yeah. Gear's packed, tanks full. I'm sorted. You headed out on the truck, or do you want to ride with me?"

"I'm down for riding with you."

"Then let's ride."

As they stepped outside into the beautiful, bright summer's day, one of the probates ran up to them. "Sir, Mr James, there's a telephone call for you."

"Is it urgent?"

"There's what sounds like a man on the line saying he has a lead for you regarding the Kloofnek fires, sir."

Nodding his thanks, Gray turned to Kyle. "Sorry, Ace, I better get this. You want to head on out on the truck rather than wait for me? I don't know how long I'll be."

"Sure, no problem. I'll see you out there."

"Yeah. Be safe." Gray went into the front office to answer the phone. "Hello?"

"Is this Grayson James?" a tinny, distorted voice asked.

"Yes, this is Grayson James. Who am I speaking to?"

"Excellent," the voice replied before the line went dead.

What the hell? Gray went looking for the probate who'd called him. Finding him helping load extra gear and supplies into one of the rescues vehicles, he stopped to ask, "Did the caller happen to give you their name?"

"No, sir. They just said they needed to talk to you urgently."

"Did they ask for me by name?"

"Yes, sir. They asked to speak to Mr Grayson James."

"And they gave you no information? Just asked for me?"

"No, sir. They just asked to speak to you because they had information about the Kloofnek fires. That's all they said."

"Okay, thanks. Appreciate it."

"No problem, sir."

Once again heading for his truck, he hit the fob to unlock as the klaxon began to blare. It looked like today was going to be one of those crazy-ass days where everything happened at once. Knowing their station was now running on skeleton staff, Gray was going to have to get his hands dirty anyway. Once again heading for the front office, he went to see where this fire was.

N o, no, no. That simply would not do! This would ruin all their plans. They needed him to be in the right place at the right time. How else were they supposed to get rid of their problem once and for all? Staring at the assembled group of men and women from their safe spot out of sight, they mumbled to themselves as they tried to come up with a plan of action. If they were to get rid of him once and for all, they would want him to be where they needed him to be. Nothing could be allowed to change the plan.

Stretching out on the sofa, Kitty groaned. Her mother had made lasagne for supper, and, as always, she'd eaten too much of it. Nobody made lasagne like her mom. Despite the gravity of her situation, she'd enjoyed having her mother with her enormously. They hadn't done this in the longest time. Since leaving home for college.

Her mom returned from doing the dishes – she hadn't been able to talk her out of it, hard as she'd tried. Taking a seat in an armchair opposite her, Kitty noticed Elenore running a maternal eye over her as she lay on the sofa, though pretended not to. She knew her mother was worried about her. It had been a pretty rough day, and in the days ahead, she was sure it would be equally as rough.

There were a lot of decisions to be made, along with a ton of arrangements. Her first priority was her staff. Thank god, she'd taken her broker's advice and invested in contingency insurance. At least salaries were covered, for her and them. One less thing to worry about on a long list of issues.

She was feeling a bit better, not quite as shattered as earlier. Hopefully, she was looking better on the outside too, not so pale and drawn. If she were honest, she'd enjoyed her evening in with her mom. She missed being at home and spending time like they had this evening. It was just what she'd needed.

"So......" Elenore began. Clearing her throat, she paused a moment, seeming to gather her thoughts.

Kitty sat up to look at her mother. "So?"

Elenore blushed. "Well, I, er......" Again, she paused.

All Kitty could do was gape. Her mother was, honest to goodness, blushing. This had to be good. She could probably count on one hand the amount of times she'd seen her mother blush in all of her twenty-eight years. And then it had only been when her father had teased her mother.

"Well, now," she said, drawing the words out. "That's interesting. Out with it, Mom. What's got you all a-tizzy?" she couldn't help teasing.

Taking a deep breath, Elenore finally said, "Well, Dad's been gone for a long time now. And you and Philip have your own lives. You don't need me as much as you used to, so I was thinking of finding myself a companion."

Kitty's father had been a wonderful man who had adored her mother. They had seemed to live their own fairy tale right up until the day he'd died. Theirs had been a happy marriage, filled with love and laughter. Like any couple, they'd had their ups and downs. But it had been a rule in the house never to go to bed angry.

She and her brother, Philip, had always known they were loved. Their parents had made sure of that. Kitty wanted the love her parents had shared for herself. And she had a sneaking suspicion it was a love she could find with Gray. In many ways, he reminded her of her dad.

They had lost him so suddenly. No one had been prepared for it, least of all her mom. He'd gotten up healthy and happy, had breakfast with her, his beloved Elenore, as usual. He'd left for work, and that was the last time they'd seen him alive. He'd suffered a sudden, massive heart attack. He'd been dead before he hit the floor, leaving his family devastated and his wife lost without him.

Now with him gone, and both she and Philip out of the house, Kitty could only imagine how lonely it must be for her mom without her darling William. In the years since he'd passed, Elenore at least had her children to focus on until they left home for college. Maybe it *was* time for some companionship for her mom. Lord knew, they pushed her about it often enough. And she might know just the man for the job.

"Ah, a companion is it? Well, you're in luck. I happen to know somebody who knows somebody."

Elenore couldn't help it. She burst out laughing. "If that's your best mafia impersonation, baby, best you stick to cupcakes."

Kitty threw a scatter cushion at her mother, snorting with laugher.

"Seriously though, Mom. I think it's long overdue. Dad would want you to be happy. There's this really nice guy who works with Gray, and I think you'd get on well. I can arrange an introduction, if you like. Think about it and let me know."

Clearly uncomfortable with the conversation, her mother replied, "Thank you, darling, I will. Now, how about some dessert? I made Baked Alaska."

"Hmm, yum. Yes, please. I'll come give you a hand." As she got to her feet, her cell phone rang.

"I'll be there in a sec, Mom."

All Gray wanted was to go home. He was tired, his body aching from constantly bracing against a hose that exerted unimaginable pressure on the body. He'd been at it for more hours than he wanted to acknowledge, and the end was nowhere near in sight. And he wanted to see Kitty.

Although she'd seemed a little less distraught when he'd seen her earlier, he'd really rather be checking in on her to make sure she was doing okay. Instead, he'd be headed back into the bowels of hell itself.

With the fire in Silvermine that had been raging for days, they were severely short-handed and being hampered at every turn. It was going to be a long, hard fight to get this blaze under control, and there was no knowing when they'd get it done. They were in it for the long haul. The warehouse currently burning housed flammable liquids, which made putting the flame out a nightmare.

And once they finally got it out, he'd have to wait just long enough for the ashes and debris to cool down before he went in to start his investigation. But for now, he had a fifteen-minute break, and he was going to use it wisely.

Pulling his cell phone out of his shirt pocket, he searched Kitty's number in his contact list and hit go. He'd better let her know what was going on. He didn't want her worrying where he was. She had enough going on as it was.

"Hello?"

Just hearing her voice made him smile. "Hey, honey."

"Gray, hi. How's it going?"

"Good, thanks. How are you feeling?"

"Quite a bit better actually. Thanks. It's done me the world of good having my mom over and just spending some time together. Like we used to do."

"That's great. I'm glad to hear it."

"So, what are you up to?"

"Well, that's actually why I'm calling."

"That doesn't sound good, Gray." Worry was clearly in Kitty's voice.

"I don't know if you've been following the news about the fire out at Silvermine."

"Yes, I heard it's been burning for days. But I haven't seen or heard any news today."

"Yeah, it's pretty much raging out of control at this point. All available manpower has been allocated to helping fight it. I was due to join the crew earlier today, but we got called out to a local fire."

Gray heard Kitty's quiet gasp. "I thought you didn't do that anymore?"

"No, I'm not on active duty anymore. But I am a volunteer. I only get called up in cases of emergency, like now. We are seriously short-staffed at the moment. All fire stations in the peninsula are running on skeleton staff."

"Please just be careful, okay?"

"I will. But I didn't call to upset you. I needed to hear your voice. Make sure that you were all right."

"I'm fine, Gray. I need you to focus on staying safe, not worrying about me. Mom's here with me, keeping me company. In fact, we decided she'll stay here with me tonight and then I'm going to pack some things and go stay with her for a few days."

"That's great, honey. I like the idea that you won't be alone. I don't know when I'm going to be getting off duty here. Once we finally manage to get this fire out, I'm going to have to go back in to start my investigation. So it gives me peace of mind knowing you're with her." Looking at his watch, Gray swore. "I've got to go, honey. My break is up."

"Please promise me you'll be careful out there, Gray."

"I promise. I have you to come home to, don't I?"

"Yes. Just make sure that you do. I miss you."

"I miss you too, baby. Take care and say hi to your mom for me.

"I will do. Bye, Gray. Come home safe."

Swallowing down the last of his now cold coffee, Gray climbed out of his truck and headed back into hell.

---

*W*asn't it magnificent? They had outdone themselves this time for sure. Flames danced, reaching higher and higher. Now all they needed to do was get him into the building. Then they could get rid of him. They needed to get rid of him. He was all that stood between them and their love. She would see he was nothing but an obstacle if they could just get him out of the picture. Without his influence, they would get their sweet girl back, and she would see that they were meant to be together. How to get him inside? How? How? Hitting a hand against the side of their head repeatedly, they continued to mumble under their breath. Stopping suddenly, they realised — that's it! Cackling softly to themselves, they set about the business of getting rid of the competition.

CHAPTER 11

Finally, they had the blaze under control. They'd managed to get hold of the manager of the company to find out what chemicals had been stored on site. Knowing what they were dealing with, they'd been able to use the correct chemicals to combat the fire and would have it out completely in no time at all.

When the last of the flames were, indeed, doused, a cheer went up. The men were tired, hot, and thirsty. And ready to call it a day. Clean up started, and Gray, along with two others, headed for the building to assess the situation on the inside.

"Guys, stay sharp. We don't know what structural damage there is, but with the intensity and duration of the fire, there will be some. Be careful in there."

The other two acknowledged him before making their way into the building and splitting up. He headed towards the back of the building to have a look at what they'd been told was the main storage area. He suspected that was where the fire had originated from.

Every few minutes, they'd each check in over their coms

to keep tabs on each other and so those outside would also know where to look for them should anything go wrong. Gray had started on one side of the back area and steadily had been working his way across when he spotted movement out of the corner of his eye.

Turning his head towards the movement, he saw someone move out of sight. Thinking it was one of his colleagues, he turned back to the task at hand. The sounds of the building settling echoed around him. Noises he was familiar with. Spotting a tell-tale pooling on the ground a little way away from him, Gray started towards it to investigate. Engaging his radio, he informed the senior on site of his suspicions of arson.

"I'm headed over to investigate now, sir."

"Copy that, James. It goes without saying, be careful in there."

"Yes, sir. You know I always am."

Suddenly, one of the I-beams near him gave off a loud screeching sound that had the hair on the back of his neck standing up. The sound any experienced fireman recognised. A sound they *feared*. Because it was the sound of danger. The metal of the hefty beam was giving a warning that it was about to fail catastrophically.

The sound that followed next had his blood running icy cold. There was no mistaking the whooshing sound of accelerant taking flame. Somebody was in there with him, and they'd just set another fire. As he started moving towards the sound of the new fire, he heard more screeching from the beam he'd just turned his back on. And he knew his time was running out. That beam wouldn't hold much longer.

Shit! Please hold just a little longer.

Engaging his coms, he notified his colleagues of his current situation. The two men in the building assured they were making their way back to assist him. All he could do was hope the beam held. But it would seem fate had other plans.

With a final bloodcurdling screech, the beam gave, toppling hundreds of kilograms in Gray's direction. He darted to his left in an attempt to avoid the falling beam. Rapidly, he ran calculations in his head, and if he was correct, the falling metal would miss him by mere millimetres. He prayed his calculations were correct.

His attention wasn't focused on the ground, and he stepped on a what felt like a bolt while at a run, losing his footing. It had, in all probability, come from the very beam hurtling towards him. Gray pitched forward, and, with the weight of his gear on his back, was unable to stop himself from falling. Fear became a living thing inside him as he fell, knowing there was no way for him to avoid being hit by the falling beam now.

His last thought was of Kitty.

Jeff Erikson had barely arrived at the scene to relieve the senior officer on site when his radio crackled to life.

"Sir, an I-beam's collapsed. The integrity of the roof is now further compromised, and I'm not sure how much longer the structure's going to hold. But, sir, James is down. He's been pinned by the beam."

Jeff's blood ran cold at the words. Gray was not only the best investigator he'd ever had the privilege to work with, but he counted him as a friend. He'd never left a man behind. Wasn't about to start now. He had no intention of losing a man on his watch.

Grabbing the radio, he barked into it, "Assess the surrounding area and report back."

The answer was quick in coming. "Shit! Sir, there's flames. There're flames. We've got a flair-up, and it's rapidly approaching the area where James is lying. Sir, we need help back here. We can't lift the beam, and there's no telling what damage he's sustained."

"Is he still alive?"

"Yes, sir. His breathing's clear, and his pulse is fairly strong. We need the flames out, and then we need a team to come and get him out."

"Right, you heard the man. Let's get those hoses to the back of the building, and let's get those flames out. If James is trapped under that beam, we're going to need time to get him out. Time we won't have if the damn building is burning. Move, move, move!"

Rubbing his hand over his tired face, Jeff sent a prayer heavenward that they'd get Gray out in time. Sprinting to the back of the building, he called for an update on the roof. He was worried that the force of the spray from the hoses would further compromise its remaining strength. The last thing he wanted was the building collapsing in on his guys.

"We can't get close enough to get a good look at it, sir. There's too much smoke up there at the moment."

"Thanks, Links. Just keep an eye on it. If it gives any indication it's gonna go, shout."

"Yes, sir."

"Okay, gentlemen, let it rip. Let's get those flames out. Pronto."

Keeping an eagle eye on everything around him, Jeff continued to direct his team. Minutes after one of his men reported the flames appeared to be doused, his radio crackled to life again. For long moments all he got was static.

". . . hear me?" distorted and faint he finally heard one of his men say.

"Say again, son? We didn't catch that."

More crackling and static, and eventually he heard words he'd prayed he wouldn't hear. "Sir, if you can hear me – she's about to come down. We can't get James out from under the beam, and there's debris already coming down from the roof. She's gonna go."

Closing his eyes, feeling physically ill knowing there was only one decision he could make, Jeff made the difficult call. "Get out, son. Do it now. I know you want to save James, but it puts you at risk too. Get out now."

"But sir, we can—"

"Get out now. That's a direct order, Marcus," Jeff cut him off.

"Yes, sir. We're coming out."

He heard the annoyed resignation in the man's voice, but what could he do? There was no other choice to be made. For the greater good. It was bad enough he had one down. It was beyond comprehension to risk another two for a very uncertain outcome.

Anxiously, he watched the doorway in the side of the building, closest to where they would have been. For what seemed an age, there was no movement. It shouldn't be taking so long. And then the first man cleared the door. As the second started to follow, the roof finally gave, and the building collapsed in on itself.

Jeff hung his head. Fear and anxiety ate at him like acid. The man trapped in that building was not just his colleague, he was a friend. Hell, the man was family! Putting in time in the trenches together, they had forged a strong bond. The worry of not knowing whether Gray was alive formed a tight knot in his stomach. And if he was, by some miracle, would he survive long enough for them to get him out?

· · ·

Jeff's nerves were stretched tight. It has seemed like forever as they'd waited for the other teams to arrive. His guys on-site had already started removing rubble. They'd barely waited for the dust to clear before they'd gotten stuck in. But there simply weren't enough hands. If Gray was, somehow, lucky enough to still be alive, he wouldn't be able to hold out for long.

There were simply too many variables in play. Was he alive? If yes, was he conscious? Could he breathe? Was he hurt? The only thing they were certain of at this point was he'd been trapped under the I-beam before the building had come down. After that? There was no knowing. Nothing else was certain.

The senior officer he'd taken over from had informed him of Gray's suspicions the fire had been arson. He'd called it in to the police department, as was his obligation as it was now considered a crime scene. He currently awaited the team they'd dispatched, along with another fire truck, the department of labour, and one or two other groups. This train wreck was now a multi-agency headache.

The search and rescue team would be bringing the necessary equipment with them. They needed the thermal imaging camera urgently. Once they got eyes on the situation below surface, they'd have a better idea of how to proceed and how best to concentrate their efforts. How much shoring would be required to prevent any further cave-ins. And they'd also have a better idea of Gray's condition.

Thankfully, the Silvermine fire was under control and men had been dispatched from there to assist with the digging.

As he watched another large chunk of debris being removed, Jeff's radio beeped, signalling its activation.

"I see them, sir. Search and Rescue just clearing the gates now."

"Thanks, Stevens. Appreciate it." Jeff was grateful Kyle Stevens had been part of the team that had arrived from Silvermine. He had a level head under pressure and knew how to get the job done.

He heard the strain in the man's voice. He knew they were all feeling it. That's what drove them to function like a well-oiled machine, working in unity to remove the rubble as quickly and efficiently as possible. When it came to one of their own, they were all in.

Once the search and rescue team was ready and in place, the team that had been digging through the ruins took a break. Kind-hearted civilians had set up a refreshment station, dishing out hot drinks and sandwiches. Kyle and the others guzzled down copious amounts of water before accepting the gift of fragrant, steaming cups of coffee. With his cup in hand, Kyle headed over to where Jeff stood talking to one of the police officers that had arrived.

"Did you need something, Stevens?"

"Sir, would it be okay if I take my thirty-minute break off-site?"

"Is it something urgent, son? Nothing that can wait?"

"It probably could, but I'd rather it didn't, if it's all the same, sir."

Something in the younger man's voice had him looking a little closer. His men were under a great amount of pressure at the moment. Whatever Jeff saw on the younger man's face had him nodding.

"All right. Thirty minutes."

"Thank you, sir."

He watched as Kyle walked away. Then he got back to the business at hand.

erking awake, Kitty reached for her cell phone to check the time. Noting it was a little past seven thirty, she was about to jump out of bed, thinking she had overslept, when she remembered there was no Decadence to go to. About to lock her screen and try to get more sleep, she saw she had a missed call. She didn't recognise the number but realised that call was probably what had woken her.

Who would be calling her at this hour of the morning? Her staff knew the score; she doubted it was one of them. Maybe it had been Gray, but she didn't recognise the number. While debating whether to call back, her phone rang in her hand.

"Hello?" Clearing the morning frog from her throat, she tried again. "Hello?"

"Hello, is this Kitty? Kitty Spence?"

Not recognising the voice, Kitty hesitated a moment before finally replying, "Yes, this is she."

"Kitty, it's Kyle. Kyle Stevens. I'm a friend of Gray's. We met that one time at your bakery?"

"Yes, I remember, Kyle. Hi."

"Kitty– er, are you home right now?"

This conversation seemed so strange. And it was starting to unsettle her. Should she admit she was at home? Chewing on the inside of her cheek, she didn't reply.

"Kitty, are you still there?"

"Yes, I'm here. I–"

"Look, I know this is so random, and you don't know me. But I need to talk to you urgently, and this is something I think needs to be said face-to-face. Are you home?"

Not really comfortable with the idea of telling him she was home, Kitty was curious as to know what brought this man to her door so early in the morning. "Yes, I'm home. Do you have the address?"

"Yeah, I have it. I'm downstairs. Can you please let me in?"

That gave her a nasty jolt. With everything that had happened, she really didn't like the idea of a total stranger knowing how to find her. Between the weird feeling of being constantly watched and Decadence being burned down, she was more than a little unsettled by this interaction with Kyle.

She had no idea who was responsible for burning down her bakery. And despite not having any proof, she was convinced that someone had been stalking her. Surely it wouldn't be Kyle though? She hadn't met him until that day when he'd accompanied Gray.

Pushing her misgivings aside, she went to let Kyle in. She just hoped she wouldn't regret it. At least she wasn't alone in the apartment, like she normally would be. If she found herself in trouble, she could always call for her mom's help.

Standing with the door slightly ajar, she heard the lift arrive on her floor. Kyle got out, and she watched him stride towards her apartment with a grim look on his handsome face. Whatever the reason he was there, she was one hundred percent sure she wasn't going to like it going by that expression. As he reached her, she stepped aside to let him in.

Stepping past her, Kyle stopped. He appeared to be waiting for her to close the door.

Doing exactly that, she said, "The living room is through here. We can talk in there." She entered the room and went to take a seat in her favourite spot. "What brings you to my door so early, Kyle?"

Lifting a hand to rub his neck, Kyle pinned her with unhappy eyes. "Are you here alone?"

Kitty didn't like this. Not one bit. Her earlier misgivings rushing back in, she took a breath before saying, "Look, Kyle, please excuse me for being rude, but it is really early in the morning. I don't know you very well. And I have no idea why you're here. So just spit it out. Okay?"

"Forgive me. I don't mean to be so mysterious, but it really would be better if you had someone here with you. I'll tell you why I'm here in a second. Do you have someone here with you?"

'Yes, my mom is here. But she's still sleeping."

"Go get her. I think you're going to need her when I tell you why I'm here."

"Oh god, is it Gray? Is something wrong with Gray? Tell me." Kitty got up from the sofa and rushed over to Kyle. "Is he hurt? Where is he? Tell me!" Kitty ended on a shout.

"We got separated on calls last night, and Gray went to assist at a warehouse fire with some of the skeleton crew, since we need all hands at the moment."

"Yes, I know. I spoke to him last night while he was on a break. What about it?"

"They finally got the fire out. Gray and two other guys went into the building to make sure they were out everywhere and to check the integrity of the structure. He would need to know that before he can go in to start his investigation."

Kitty heard her mother. "Pussycat, is everything all right? Why are you shouting?" Spotting Kyle, she stopped, her hand reaching to smooth her hair. She pulled the lapels of her dressing gown a little closer. "I'm sorry. I didn't realise you had company. Is everything all right? I hope I'm not interrupting."

"No, Mom, you're not. This is Kyle. He's a friend of Gray's. He was just telling me why he's here."

Moving to stand beside her daughter, Elenore wrapped an arm around Kitty's shoulders but said no more.

Turning back to Kyle, Kitty prompted, "Yes?"

Blowing a harsh breath out through his mouth, Kyle

looked Kitty square in the eyes. "Kitty... I– Shit! This is hard. Sorry. It's just– There was– An I-beam collapsed on Gray. And before they could get him out—"

"No! Don't say it." The words ripped out of Kitty before she even realised she'd said a word.

"Kitty, the building– It collapsed before they could get him out. I need to get back. We're busy moving rubble so we can get to him. But I wanted to come tell you first. I didn't want you to hear it from anyone else, maybe on the news."

Shock and fear held her in a painful grip. Stumbling back to the sofa, she sat down. She never said a word. Couldn't get a word out. The words seemed to be trapped in her throat along with the bubble of hysteria she was trying really hard not to let escape. She was terrified if she opened her mouth, all that hysteria would come bubbling forth.

"I'm sorry, Kitty." Kyle took her hand. "We know the risk we take when we pull on the uniform. It's a choice we make. Our family and friends, they accept it only because they love us. But it's hard on them. Especially at times like this."

"Please, Kyle, bring him home. Please?"

"I promise to do my damnedest to make it happen. I have to get back now, but I'll be in touch." With a gentle squeeze of the hand he held, Kyle rose.

"I'll see you out," Elenore said, leading him to the door. Kitty sat exactly in the same position as when her mother had escorted Kyle to the door. She felt Elenore pull her into an embrace and let herself relax into it.

"I'm so sorry, Pussycat," she heard her mother whisper.

Sitting like that for a while, Kitty drew comfort from her mother's presence. Her mind reeled with all that had happened to her in the last couple of days. She'd lost her business, but she could rebuild that. What if she lost Gray too? It didn't bear thinking that she could lose him before they even had a chance to explore where these feelings between them could go.

Yes! We did it. We warned you, Mr Fire Investigator. You wouldn't listen. Now you are gone, and she is all ours again. Just as it should be.

Standing amongst the crowd that had gathered as the workday was beginning, they watched as the rescue crew worked to remove the rubble to get to the trapped man. Excited chatter from the onlookers centred around what was going on. Speculation was rife. But they knew. And they rejoiced.

CHAPTER 12

Kitty sat glued to the television. It had been hours, and she'd barely moved. Was too afraid to move in case she missed something. The fire had made the national news, so there were reporters on scene reporting live. It seemed a nation was holding its collective breath to hear whether the "firefighter trapped beneath the rubble" would be rescued. It was still uncertain whether he was alive, but he had a nation praying he was.

Sitting in her living room, Kitty felt like she was losing her mind. There'd been no news from Kyle yet. Apparently, they'd not yet managed to remove enough rubble to determine Gray's status. That constant worry gnawed at her – the not knowing. Would she ever get to see that beautiful smile he saved especially for her again? Feel the sheer bliss of those strong arms holding her tight? Taste his passion as he kissed her?

Why was this happening? Not just to them but to Gray specifically. He brought so much good to the world. So much brightness. It felt like they were being punished. As if this budding relationship wasn't being given a chance at all. *Please God, let him be okay?*

Pulling her legs up, Kitty rested her chin on her knees. Wrapping her arms tightly around herself, she continued to watch the screen. So absorbed in what she was watching, she never heard the gate buzzer or her mom letting visitors in. Morgan and Leyla rushed into the room.

"Hey, precious. Mom called, and we rushed right over," Morgan said. Dropping to the seat beside her, she pulled Kitty into her arms, hugging her tight.

"Hey, babes. We got here as soon as we could," Lee added, taking a seat on the coffee table in front of her, looking uncomfortable.

Resting her aching head on Morgan's shoulder, she looked at Lee with tired, aching eyes. "Thanks for coming, but it wasn't necessary."

"Of course it was. Why on earth would you say that? We know you're hurting; where else would we be when you need us?" Morgan replied.

Lee never said a word. Simply nodded her agreement.

"Thank you, loves. I know I can always count on the two of you." Kitty sighed. "I must look a frightful sight."

"Come then. Let's get you in the shower and some food into you. I'm sure you'll feel a bit better after that."

By the time Kitty got out of the shower, she was feeling a little more human, if not much better. Her tired brain kept looping through the thought that she wasn't ready for the possible outcome of this horrible situation. She and Gray were only getting started, and it could already be over.

Then a chilling thought popped into her head, stilling her

hand as she tugged a brush through her wet hair. Could she do this every day? For a lifetime? If, by some miracle, Gray survived this and their relationship deepened, could she go through this fear every time he went to work? Danger was part of his job. Could she learn to live with it? Or would it consume her a little more each time he walked out the door?

She needed to give it some thought. As much as she was attracted to Gray, loved spending time with him, talking to him, she wasn't sure she could do this. She wasn't sure she was strong enough.

Taking a couple of pain pills to help with the headache that was the result of all the tears and tension of the day, she gave herself one last look in the mirror. Time she got back to the others before they came looking for her.

She walked into the living room to find all three ladies sitting watching the television. The look on their faces told her all she needed to know. There'd been no good news while she'd been getting cleaned up. When her mom spotted her standing in the doorway, she got to her feet.

"I'll make you some toast and scrambled egg." Opening her mouth to decline the food, her mother beat her to it. "You need to eat something. You'll make yourself sick if you don't."

Knowing it was pointless to argue, she simply nodded. Her mother headed for the kitchen. Taking her usual spot on the sofa, Kitty curled her legs under her as she sat.

"There you go, Pussycat. Eat up." Her mom handed her a plate and cutlery.

"Thanks, Mom."

Taking a bite, Kitty bit back a moan. She hadn't thought she was hungry until she put that first forkful of fluffy eggs in her mouth. Suddenly, she was ravenous. Wolfing down the rest of the eggs, she cleaned her plate in no time. Her mother took the plate from her, handing her a steaming mug of coffee.

The ringing of her cell phone had her jumping at the unexpectedness of it.

With a shaking hand, she answered it. "Hello?"

"Kitty, hey. It's Kyle. I wanted to give you a heads up. We're about to break through the rubble. We're pushing back the barriers so they can't film it, but it won't take them long to get their hands on the news and broadcast it. I'd rather you heard it from me than them."

Her heart thumped with anxiety. It felt like a tiny bird trapped in her chest. She wondered if that's how it felt at the start of a heart attack.

"Thanks, Kyle. I appreciate it."

"It's all good. Stay on the line with me, yeah?"

"Yeah."

Kyle was silent for some time, but she could hear him breathing on the other side. She took the opportunity to let the others know what was going on.

Finally, she heard, "Yes! They're through. We're lucky that the way the building collapsed, there's a big enough clearance in the rubble to get to him. They're sending someone down."

Please, god, let him be okay. Please? Don't let him die down there.

"Okay." Was all she could manage. It felt like a boulder had lodged in her throat. Between the pounding of her heart and suddenly finding it difficult to draw a breath, Kitty was almost convinced she was having a heart attack.

It seemed like it was taking forever. Why was it taking so long, damn it? Surely, they should have reached him by now. Reaching out, she gripped Morgan's hand. Holding on as if Morgan was all that anchored her in place, she waited, barely breathing for word to come.

After what seemed like hours, she heard a radio crackle to life on the other end of the line. She couldn't make out what was being said, but then an almighty cheer went up. And then she heard Kyle's shout of jubilation.

"They found him, Kitty. And he's alive."

Kitty could hear the emotion in Kyle's voice. Realisation dawned that despite telling her otherwise, he'd been convinced they'd find Gray dead underneath all the rubble. He'd known, better than her, the odds that had been stacked against finding him alive and well. Yet he'd chosen to offer her hope in the face of his own fears.

Tears of relief tracked down her face. "Thank you, Kyle. For everything. For trying to make this situation easier for me, even when you knew things were grim. I really do appreciate it."

"Under different circumstances, I'd say it's a pleasure. I'm just grateful I could give you good news. Oh, hang on a sec." Kitty heard him speak to someone else before continuing. "Senior on site has just informed me it'll be approximately another ten minutes before we can haul him out. They'll assess his condition before they can move him. But once we can move him, he's being sent to Foreshore General Hospital. I'll let you know when we're en route. You can meet us there."

"Okay, thanks. I'll do that. See you there in approximately an hour then?"

"Yeah. An hour sounds good."

Now impatient, Kitty jumped to her feet. Her mother, Morgan, and Lee stood with her.

"What's going on, Pussycat?" her mother asked, taking in her agitation.

"They've found him. Oh my god, they found him. He's alive." Her voice hitched as she fought to hold it together.

"Apparently, they need to assess him before they can move him. But once they've checked him over, they're taking him to Foreshore General. I'm meeting Kyle there."

Dashing towards the emergency room doors, Kitty's eyes darted around, frantically searching for Kyle. Not seeing him outside or in the parking lot, she ran for the doors. She spotted him as she cleared the entry. Thankful, she rushed over to him.

"Hi, Kyle. Any news yet?"

"Hey. Nothing yet. The ER doc is doing his own assessment at the moment. His pulse, blood pressure, and heart rate all appear to fine. What's got them concerned is there's no way of knowing how long he was unconscious and if he suffered lack of air at any point."

"Lack of air? Didn't he have his breathing apparatus?"

"Yeah, he had it. But his mask got knocked off at some point. We just don't know when. There's no way to tell. So, they're sending him for an MRI to see what's going on with his brain. You're going to want to get comfortable. It's going to be a long wait."

Try as she might, a tiny sob still managed to escape.

"Hey now," Kyle said, pulling her into a hug. "He's in really good hands. He'll be fine."

Nodding but not saying anything, she allowed Kyle's warmth and confidence to calm her. Her mother and two friends were just entering the emergency room as she stepped out of his embrace. They made their way over to where she stood.

Introductions over, Kyle led them to a quiet waiting room a little way down the passage, away from the frenetic pace of the emergency room. Making sure they were comfortable, he excused himself to get an update on Gray's situation. Despite the small size of the room, Kitty paced. There was no way she could sit quietly waiting to hear news. After a couple of hours in the waiting room, she told the others it wasn't necessary for them to stay.

"We've no idea how long this is going to take, and I don't expect you to sit here with me. I know you guys have to work in the morning."

"It's okay, babes. We'll hang for a while longer," Lee answered for both of them, Morgan nodding her agreement.

Knowing it was pointless to argue, they'd stay regardless, she turned to her mom. "You still hanging in there, Mom?"

"Yes, my sweet girl. The question is, are you?"

"Yeah, I guess. I mean, I never gave any thought to being in a situation like this. Now that I am, I'm not sure what to do with it. This is hard. But, for the most part, I guess I'm hanging in there."

Seeing the worried look her mother gave, Kitty quickly turned her attention back to Morgan and Lee. There'd been more to the look than merely concern, more that she wasn't ready to get into.

A little after one in the morning, Kyle came in bearing coffee. Giving Kitty a half smile, he said, "They've done all the tests they're able to do for now, so he'll be going up to the ward in a few minutes. I told the floor sister you're his fiancée, so she's agreed to allow you to stay with him."

Choking on the mouthful of coffee she'd just taken, Kitty wiped at her watering eyes while nodding her thanks. Clearing her throat, she replied, "Thanks, Kyle. You've been an enormous support today. I can't thank you enough."

Resting his hand on her shoulder, he gave it a gentle squeeze. "It's all good. Gray would have done the same for me had the roles been reversed. I have to get back to work now that the imminent danger is over. But I'll pop in again once my shift is over. If you need anything, don't hesitate to give me a call."

"I will. Thanks again."

"Stay strong. I'll see you later." With a last smile, he headed for the door.

His hand on the handle, Kitty called out to him.

"Be safe, Kyle. One down is plenty enough. Take care, okay?"

"Will do, ma'am." He gave her a two-fingered salute.

Before he could close the door, one of the nurses escorting Gray up to the ward popped her head around the corner to let them know they were taking him up.

"Thank you. I'll be right there," she replied to the lady.

"It's probably best if you head on home. You won't be able to stay with me in the ward, and there's no point in sitting here staring at the walls," Kitty then addressed her mom and friends.

"All right, love. Keep us up to date, yeah?"

"I will do, Morgs." With tears in her eyes, Kitty hugged her mom, Morgan, and Lee in turn. "Thank you for everything, guys. I wouldn't have made it through without you."

Morgan pulled her in for another hug. For a long moment, Kitty clung to her lifelong friend, taking comfort in her embrace. Then, taking a quiet breath for strength, Kitty followed Gray's bed as they wheeled it to the elevator.

***

The room was in utter disarray. Their anger knew no bounds. He was supposed to have died! But no, somehow the bastard had managed to survive not only being trapped in a burning building but having the building collapse on him. Was there no getting rid of this man? What did they have to do to get him out of the way? If they were ever to get their girl, they needed him gone. Permanently. But how? They had done some of their absolute best work on this one, yet he was still alive. Picking up yet another object close to hand, they hurled it across the room with all the might of their rage. They would find a way.

CHAPTER 13

Slowly, Gray slipped into consciousness. He lay quietly for a bit, absorbing the sounds around him. He knew instantly he wasn't home, but where the hell was he? Then he heard it. The tell-tale beep of a heart monitor.

Shit! He was in the hospital. With no recollection of how he got there. The last he remembered, he, Marcus, and Links had been in the warehouse. Then the I-beam had fallen on him, and he didn't remember anything after that.

Taking a moment, he took stock of how he felt. No pain, thankfully. He knew that would be pain meds. It wouldn't last. But while it did, he was going to enjoy the benefits. His brain was a bit fuzzy, and his tongue felt thick in his mouth. He had a raging thirst.

Opening his eyes, he let them roam. Around the room, then over his body. Seeing his left leg suspended, encased in a cast, he idly wondered how bad the break was. He didn't see anything other than that though.

Hearing a soft sigh, he turned his head towards the sound. Kitty lay with her head on her folded hands resting on the edge of the bed, asleep. His heart squeezed at the sight of her. God, she was beautiful. Her cheeks were stained the lightest rose pink, her lashes creating crescent shadows where they lay against her skin.

Unable to resist, he reached out his hand to catch a curl around his finger. Rubbing it between thumb and finger as the lock clung lovingly to his skin, he marvelled in the silky texture.

Another sigh drew his gaze back to her face. Seeing her eyelashes flutter, he steeled himself for the impact of looking into her beautiful, hazel-green eyes. Eyes that had a way of making you feel like she could see all the way into a man's soul.

Slowly, they opened. Gray felt a ripple of awareness — he wanted to wake up to those gorgeous jade and amber orbs every day for the rest of his life. He'd been given a second chance at life, and he wanted to spend it with her.

Before he could give voice to his thoughts, her gaze met his, and all thought stalled as he got lost there. Lost in the warm intensity in her eyes.

"You're awake." She straightened as she spoke. Grimacing as obviously cramped muscles protested.

"Yeah," he croaked, his voice hoarse from the smoke inhalation.

Taking her hand in his, he gave her a goofy smile. There was so much he wanted to say to her, things he'd come to understand as he'd lain there watching her sleep. But before he could utter a word, he heard a noise from the door.

Both Gray and Kitty turned to see the doctor enter the room.

"Good morning, Mr James, Mrs James. I'm Dr Russo." The doctor smiled. "I'm glad to see you're awake, Mr James. How are you feeling this morning?"

Hearing the doctor call Kitty "Mrs James" caused a pang in the region of his heart. He liked the sound of that.

"Like something fell on me," Gray quipped.

Laughing at the wisecrack, the doctor answered, "I can only imagine. Feeling any pain?"

Gray shook his head. He was grateful, because he knew that when he did, he was going to be in a world of hurt.

"Good to know our superior drugs are working then."

Grinning at the doctor's comment, he asked, "So how bad is it, doc?"

The doctor's face sobered. "Mr James, you are one lucky man. I cannot believe how minimal your injuries are considering everything that happened to you. Other than some smoke inhalation and that broken leg, you're fine. A few weeks in the cast to heal, some intense physio to get the leg working one hundred percent, and you'll be back at work in no time."

"How bad's the break then?"

"There's two breaks in the left femur. You are very lucky they're such clean breaks. They should heal with absolutely no problems."

"Always a silver lining, right, doc?"

"Yes, I guess. Actually, that's a pretty good way to look at it. I'll have the physiotherapist look in on you sometime later to have a chat regarding the way forward. Well, I'm off to finish my rounds. I'll check in on you again this evening."

"Thanks, Dr Russo."

The doctor left, and Gray turned to Kitty. Even tired and clearly stressed, she was still the most beautiful woman he'd ever laid eyes on.

"How are you doing, honey?"

Looking a bit taken aback at the question, she gave a little laugh and shook her head.

"I should be asking you that. In fact, I *am* asking that. How are *you* doing?"

"Feeling a bit like I've swallowed a desert, but otherwise I'm feeling okay right now. That'll probably change once the meds wear off. But I'm good for now."

"Can I get you anything?"

"Something to drink would be great, thanks."

Getting up, Kitty poured a glass of ice water a nurse had brought in while the doctor had been talking to Gray. Handing it to him, she smoothed a hand over his forehead where a lock had fallen. Ignoring the glass in his hand, he leaned into the touch. Savoured the feel of her cool hand on his skin.

The simple touch had him feeling like he was suddenly in free fall. He didn't recognise the sensation immediately. But when he did, his heart clenched. Just as it had when the doctor had addressed Kitty as Mrs James. In that instant, it became abundantly clear what the feeling was. Love. Pure and simple. He was in love with Kitty. In the time it had taken for him to draw a breath, his life had changed.

Looking up at her, he saw tears gather in her eyes.

"Hey now. What's this?"

Shaking her head, Kitty took a moment to answer.

"Sorry. I..." The words faltered as she choked back a sob.

Reaching for the hand still cupped around his face, he laced his fingers through hers.

"Talk to me, love. Tell me what's got you so upset?"

Her mouth opened and closed a couple of times, but no words came out. Gray watched as emotion chased across her pale face. Realising just how pale she was, he took a moment to really study her.

Understanding bloomed uncomfortably in his stomach. If he wasn't so out of it with drugs pumping through his system, he'd have clued in sooner. Of course she was upset.

He could only imagine the anguish she'd been through. For them, it was all part of the job. For their loved ones, it was a lot harder. Raising the bed into a more upright position, Gray pulled Kitty into his embrace as best he could. Which was somewhat uncomfortable since she stood on the same side his leg was in a sling.

"Oh honey, I'm sorry. That was a bit slow of me."

Shaking her head again, Kitty still said nothing. Seemingly couldn't speak through the sobs now racking her body. Tightening his arms around her, Gray placed gentle kisses on her head as she burrowed into his embrace and gave vent to emotions that had obviously been bottled up.

***

God, this man! He'd been through hell and back, but all he was concerned about was her. Could he possibly be any sweeter?

Kitty curled farther into his embrace, accepting the comfort he so readily offered, crying harder. So overcome with the emotions of the past two days she couldn't keep it bottled up anymore. It demanded to be released, acknowledged, soothed. It would no longer be denied.

She should be the one who was being strong for him. But he showed no signs of needing it. Still, she felt selfish even as she took from him. Finally getting a grip on herself, Kitty slowly pulled back out his arms. Standing up straight, she searched for something to wipe her wet face. She shuddered to think what she must look like. No makeup, red nose, and puffy eyes.

"Thanks, Gray, but I'm okay now." Swiping a tissue under her nose again, she continued, "Drink some of your water before the ice melts completely."

"Don't worry about the ice, Kitty. Talk to me."

"I'm fine now. Sorry. It's been a rough couple of days. For everyone, I guess."

"I don't care about everyone else, damn it! I only care about you. I know what you've just been through isn't easy. Just talk to me," Gray ground out through gritted teeth, clearly annoyed.

She was completely taken aback by Gray's apparent anger. Had yet to experience this side of him directed at her. The only time she'd seen him in any kind of bad mood had been over the fires being set by an arsonist in Kloofnek. And she found she didn't like it. Not one bit.

To be fair though, he'd been through one hell of an ordeal. And now he was having to deal with her breaking down. She should be taking care of him. Not the other way around. Drawing a breath to tell him just that, something on her face must have given her away, because he spoke first.

"Don't. Don't even say what's you're thinking. I'm not interested in hearing that bullshit. I know the risk I take when I put that uniform on each day. I signed up for this. You didn't. This just landed in your lap."

Huffing out the breath she'd just taken, Kitty realised arguing was pointless.

"Fine. What do you want me to say, Gray?"

"How about being honest with me about what you're feeling?"

"You sure you want to hear how I'm feeling?" she snapped back, her own anger stirring to life.

"I wouldn't ask if I didn't want to. You can't keep it bottled up, Kitty. It's not healthy."

"So, you want me to tell you that I felt like I was losing my mind, thinking I might never get to see you again?" As she spoke, anger took a deeper hold. She was tired and seriously not in the mood for this. "Or would you prefer me to tell you I felt like a piece of me was slowing dying as I sat glued to the

TV, hour after hour, as I waited for news? Any news." She paused to take a breath. "What exactly would you like me to say, hmm?"

"Kitty, honey–"

On a roll now, she spoke right over him.

"Or would you rather I tell you about the agony of waiting on the phone with Kyle as they broke through the rubble, about to find out if you were still alive or if you were dead? Knowing the chances of life were slim, but praying with everything in me that you would be alive?" Breathing hard now, she stopped.

Gray gave no answer. But his gaze never wavered from hers.

"Well?"

Looking at him, Kitty felt her anger fade away as quickly as it had appeared as she took in the stricken expression on Gray's face. A sick feeling of shame took its place. Reaching for his hands, she held them to her as she looked into his eyes. But she couldn't hold his gaze as she saw the pain her thoughtless words had caused him.

"I'm sorry, Gray," she whispered. "That was thoughtless and uncalled for."

Finally, he spoke. "It's okay, honey. I shouldn't have pushed." He squeezed her hands gently.

"No, it's not okay. You were only expressing your concern, and I behaved like a spoilt child with a broken toy. I really am sorry."

One of the nurses came bustling in, a clipboard under her arm, a smile on her face.

"Mr James, lovely to see you're back with us. How are you feeling?"

Seeing an opportunity to escape for a short while, Kitty said, "I'm going to get some coffee at the shop downstairs. Can I get you anything?"

Shaking his head, Gray never said anything. But his eyes remained on her. It felt as if they were burning a hole in her skin. She *knew* he wanted to say more. She could see it on his face. But he wouldn't in front of the nurse. Making good her escape while she could, Kitty placed a gentle kiss on his forehead saying, "I'll be back in a few."

Walking toward the lifts, she chided herself for her poor behaviour. Worry and lack of sleep had her temper frayed, but that was no excuse for the way she'd laid into Gray. He didn't deserve it. He'd been more concerned about her than himself, and she'd thrown it back in his face.

If anything, she should have been the one to ask him how he was doing. Should have been the one to offer emotional support to him. Not the other way around. She needed to figure out a way to make it up to him.

She needed coffee, tons of coffee. And a good night's sleep – something she hadn't had in three nights. Since this whole ordeal had started.

The cheerful coffee and gift shop in the hospital foyer gave Kitty's spirits a little lift as she entered the brightly lit space. Looking around, one wouldn't think it was housed in a hospital at all. A balm to her rather tattered emotions. She walked over to the counter to order her coffee, waiting her turn in the short queue.

"Good morning, ma'am. What can I get for you?" A lovely smile accompanied the words.

"Good morning. I'd like a large latte to go, please." She couldn't help but smile back at the young man behind the counter.

"A large latte, to go," he repeated her order. "Will that be all, ma'am?"

"Yes, thanks. That's all."

She handed him the money, looking around the space as she waited for him to complete the transaction.

"There we are. Thank you." He handed her the change. "Your coffee will be but a moment. You're welcome to take a seat while you wait."

Smiling her thanks, Kitty wandered over to a display of bright flower arrangements. A young woman was taking some off a trolley to add to the display, filling in the gaps. Kitty smiled at her before turning to take a seat while waiting for her coffee.

"Excuse me?"

Kitty turned. The young woman held a beautiful, bright pink Gerbera daisy out toward her.

"Such a pretty lady shouldn't look so sad. This is for you." She gestured to the flower in her hand. "I hope it will cheer you up."

Feeling the burn of tears, Kitty blinked. "Thank you. It's beautiful. You're very kind."

"I hope it brightens your day."

She went back to packing flowers on the display shelf. Kitty dashed the lone tear that escaped away.

"Ma'am, your coffee is ready," the cashier called out.

Collecting her coffee, she smiled at the cashier and again at the flower lady. Walking past the flowers, an idea struck. Was it unusual to buy flowers for a man?

"Excuse me, but how much for the yellow daisies?" Kitty asked the salesclerk.

Paying her the appropriate amount, Kitty left the shop with her coffee, her flower, and a bold bouquet of yellow daisies in a matching square, transparent glass vase for Gray.

Waiting for the lift to arrive, she contemplated how much better that small interaction had made her feel. The ragged edges felt a little smoother, a little less frayed. With a better handle on her emotions, she would apologise to Gray again when she got back and hope the daisies not only brought out that gorgeous smile of his but aided in her apology.

When she got back to the room, however, she found he had visitors. She recognised the older gentleman in the group as the senior officer on scene the night Decadence had burned down. She'd also encountered him a time or two after. She really liked him. She didn't recognise the other two men with him though.

"Kitty, there you are, honey." Gray held out a hand to her. She set down the flowers and coffee. As she took his hand, he continued, "You remember Jeff Erikson?"

"Yes, I remember Jeff. How are you?"

"All the better for seeing your lovely face," he quipped. "And you brought me flowers, I see."

Everyone laughed. Kitty blushed and stated, "I thought their sunniness might cheer Gray's skies."

Jeff replied, "Your beauty was all he needed for that."

"Hey now. I'm still in the room, Casanova," Gray interjected. Again, everyone got a big laugh. "Thank you, Kitty, for the flowers." The look in his eyes told Kitty he had more to say about them later.

Jeff's expression turned solemn and he continued, "Seriously though, I'm happier now that I can see our boy's doing just fine." He paused, shifting on his feet and clearing his throat, appearing a bit emotional for a moment, but then, "And it seems, from what I can see, he'll be back to give me more grey hair in no time at all. Of that I have no doubt."

Laughing at Jeff because the man couldn't be serious for long, Gray gestured to the other two men.

"These other two reprobates are Kevin Links and Roger Marcus. They were working with me during the accident."

It gave Kitty a nasty jolt to be reminded of the reason they were all there. It still had her blood running cold every time she thought about it. She would be eternally thankful it had such a positive outcome. An outcome that could so easily have been far more devastating.

Putting on her game face, she smiled at the two men.

"It's lovely to meet you both."

The taller of the two men, Kevin, spoke first. "Likewise, ma'am. I wish it was under different circumstances though."

"Agreed," said Roger. Clearly a man of few words.

---

*P*acing the confines of their room, they continued to rail against the fates. How is it they'd done everything right and still he continued to live, plaguing them? All they'd ever wanted was life with their love. But nothing they did made that damn fire investigator go away. Would he forever be the bane of their life? What more could they do to get rid of him? Railing turned to contemplation as they continued to pace back and forth. There had to be a way. They would figure it out. Their future depended on it.

CHAPTER 14

Stress was her faithful companion. Constantly it gnawed at her.

Kitty was worried about getting Decadence back up and running. People were relying on her. Yes, the insurance was currently paying out so they all continued to receive a wage, but that wouldn't last forever. She needed to get back to work. Besides everything else, it was her stress reliever.

She worried about Gray too. He still hadn't said a word about the ordeal he'd been through. She didn't believe he was fine and that nothing relating to the incident bugged him. Surely bottling all that up couldn't be healthy. Didn't they have policies in place that forced them to see someone, to talk about the trauma? To deal with the emotions in play?

Fear — it was a living, breathing thing inside her. When she closed her eyes at night, she relived all the agonising hours she'd gone through. Fear of the unknown – was he alive or dead? Injured or fine? And what happened when he was cleared to return to active duty? She would have to live with it daily, always wondering if that day would be the last she would see him as she kissed him goodbye.

Kitty pulled into the parking lot of the hospital for the last time. She was thankful Gray was coming home today. She loathed hospitals. Since he lived in a house, they'd agreed it would be best if she came to stay with him rather than him staying in her small flat. She would take care of him for the first few weeks.

She greeted a couple of his colleagues she recognised on her way to the lifts. His room had been a hive of activity. Colleagues popped in at random times to see how he was doing. The nurses on the floor were loving all the handsome, buff men passing through their doors. The thought of even the rather dour senior floor sister succumbing to a bit of flirting had Kitty smiling.

"Good morning, gorgeous! What's got you all smiles today?" Gray asked, as Kitty stepped into the room.

"I saw a couple of your colleagues leaving as I arrived. It made me think of how they've managed to make even Sister McMillan crack a smile or two. Your bunch are complete incorrigible."

"Seemed an almost impossible feat too."

Narrowing her eyes at him, Kitty asked, "What did you do?"

Laughing, Gray gave her his best innocent expression. "Why would you think I did anything?"

"Because I know you."

"I'm *almost* ashamed to admit we made a small wager."

Batting him on the arm, Kitty shook her head. "Like I said, incorrigible!"

"You have superb timing, by the way."

"I do?"

"Yep. Doc's been in to give the go ahead to leave. I've just finished signing the paperwork. I cannot wait to get the hell out of here."

"Well then, let's not delay. Let me grab your things, and we'll head for home."

Gray, who'd been in the process of wrangling his crutches, stilled. He turned to her, a funny look on his face.

"What? Did I say something wrong?" Kitty asked.

"No. Not a thing. I like the sound of that is all."

The way he said it made Kitty wonder what he was leaving unsaid. She put his duffel bag down on the bed. Turning toward the door, she spoke over her shoulder.

"I'll be right back," she said. "I'll go let them know we're leaving."

A few minutes later, both Kitty and a nurse were back, the nurse pushing a wheelchair.

Carefully coming to his feet, Gray looked indignantly at it.

"Oh hell no. I'm not getting in that thing."

"I'm sorry, sir. If you want to go home, I'm afraid you're going to have to hop in." The nurse smiled kindly at him. "It's hospital procedure."

With a pained expression on his face, Gray complied.

By the time they got back to Gray's house, Kitty could see he was visibly flagging. Her heart hurt to see this vital man so fatigued after nothing more than a car ride.

Using his house keys he'd found in his bag, Gray opened the garage door. Wordlessly, she parked the car and climbed out. While he opened his door, she grabbed his crutches out the back.

Slowly, painfully, he made his way into the house. Kitty followed with his bag. Making his way into the living room, Gray carefully lowered himself onto the sofa. By the time he'd managed it, his face was pale and perspiring. She could see him gritting his teeth, but he never uttered a word.

Kitty knew he'd been incredibly lucky to have only broken a leg in the cave-in. His body, however, had taken quite the beating from the debris that had rained down on him. The pain of moving his abused body was clearly stamped on his face. She wished she could take it from him. As it was, the best she could do was settle him as comfortably as she could in front of the television.

"I have some calls to make and emails to send. Can I get you anything before I start?" she asked Gray.

"No, thanks. I'm good for now. I'm just going to lie here and watch something. Maybe get a bit of shuteye."

"All right. Let me know if you change your mind."

Hauling her laptop out of the bag she'd brought in with her, Kitty made herself comfortable on the other sofa. Becoming engrossed in what she was doing, it was sometime later that she looked over to check on Gray. At some point, he'd obviously succumbed to the fatigue and was sleeping deeply, it appeared. So as not to disturb him, she quietly left the room to make her calls.

Every part of him wept in agony. The medication they'd given him in the hospital had clearly worn off. Gritting his teeth, Gray shifted, trying to find a more comfortable position. After a couple minutes of trying and failing miserably, he gave up. Lying still, he listened for Kitty, wondering where she'd disappeared to.

Not hearing a sound coming from anywhere in the house, he sighed. Damn, he needed the bathroom desperately. As he was trying to get to his feet, Kitty came into the room.

"What are you doing?"

Gray's head jerked back before swinging toward her.

"Good god, woman! Give a guy a bit of warning."

"Sorry. I didn't mean to startle you. The question, however, still remains. What are you doing?"

"What does it look like I'm doing?"

"Fine, smartass. Where are you going?"

"I gotta go."

"Okay, fair enough. But why didn't you call for me?"

"Because I'm used to doing for myself, Kitty. It's an adjustment having to rely on other people for help." Exasperation was clear in his voice.

Sighing, Kitty replied, "I can imagine it would be. Sorry, I didn't mean to snap."

"I'm sorry too. I guess this is going to take more adjusting than I thought."

"Come on then. Let's get you up so you can do what you need to do."

Getting Gray to his feet using the method they'd shown her in the hospital proved to be easier than either of them had anticipated. Once up, Kitty handed him his crutches. He hobbled off as fast as was safe.

When he got back from the bathroom, Kitty had disappeared again. He hadn't thought his house was that big. But at this rate, he was going to have to put a tracking device on the confounded woman.

"Kitty?"

"I'm in the kitchen. Trying to figure out what to make for dinner."

Laughing, he replied, "Yeah, good luck with that. Supplies were running low even before I ended up in the hospital."

"I suppose you could say that. Personally, I thought pretty sad and empty were good words to describe the state of your cupboards and fridge."

With another snort of laughter, he rested against the doorframe. Just stood there, taking in the sight of Kitty in his kitchen. With a pang in the region of his heart, he realised how right it felt. That in that moment, he was right where he was meant to be. *They* were right where they were meant to be.

The sight of Kitty bending over to check the contents of a cupboard completely derailed any further thought as all blood rushed south. That perfectly plump, rounded ass had him itching to get his hands on it.

Clearing his throat, Gray tightened his grip on the handles of his crutches.

"Er, Kitty..."

"Hmm?"

"Could you maybe not do that right now?"

Frowning, she looked over at him. "Not do what?"

"Not bend over like that right now."

"I'm sorry. Am I missing someth–" He saw her gaze drop. "Oh."

"Yeah. Oh. And there's not much I can do about it. So, I'd be very grateful if you could, you know, just not. Please?"

He hadn't meant for it to come out like he was begging. But at this point, if it meant she'd quit waving her fine ass in his face, he'd beg.

Straightening, she turned to look at him fully. She rounded the island counter and headed his way. He wasn't sure the gleam in her eye meant anything good. Coming to stop in front of him, she smoothed her hands across his chest. The little humming sound she made at the back of her throat definitely didn't help.

"How about we head back to the living room and see if we can make you a little more... comfortable?" The smile Kitty gave Gray was pure seduction.

Yep, there it was. What that gleam in her eye had meant. Moving past him, she sashayed her way to the living room door. Using the doorframe for support, he watched the show. At the other doorway, she turned and gave him another one of those smiles before disappearing into the room.

Grabbing his crutches, Gray made to follow. He'd taken no more than a few steps when the doorbell rang. He swore. Ripely, and with much enthusiasm.

"I'll get it," Kitty called out.

Making his way farther down the passage, he heard her talking to someone. As he reached the doorway, he saw it was Kyle. While Gray was genuinely fond of his friend, in that moment, he wasn't feeling it.

<hr>

Carrying multiple bags of groceries into the kitchen from the garage, Kitty had to use her foot to close the dividing door. She spotted Kyle at the fridge, a beer and a soda in his hands. When Kyle spotted her, he put the items on the counter to give her a hand.

"Here, let me take those from you."

"Thanks, Kyle. I didn't realise that one bag was so heavy."

"Why didn't you rather make two trips?"

"Ha! Two trips? Never. No self-respecting shopper makes two trips unless there is absolutely no other option."

"You nutter." Laughing, he headed over to collect his and Gray's drinks off the counter.

"What can I say? You've found me out," Kitty quipped in response. "Will you be joining us for dinner this evening?"

"Like for a home-cooked meal?" Kyle appeared taken aback by the offer.

"Yes, like a home-cooked meal."

"Hell yeah, I'm in," he replied. "If it's not an imposition."

"Of course not, silly. I only asked because I don't know

what your plans are. And so I don't make too little if you were staying."

"Then I'm definitely in."

"Okay, great. Now, I still need to pack these groceries away before I can get started with dinner, so scram. Go beat Gray at games or yell at a sports game or something."

Laughing at her teasing, he offered her a bow and that smile that usually had the ladies swooning. "Yes, ma'am. Consider me gone."

The meal over, Kyle refused to allow Kitty to do the dishes. He'd cleared the dining room table, rinsed off the plates, and loaded the dishwasher. The men had fallen on the simple meal of homemade chicken and mushroom pie, mashed potatoes, and gravy like they hadn't seen food in weeks. So, while Kyle cleaned up, Kitty helped Gray get comfortable on the couch before heading to Gray's study to call her mom.

Entering what was clearly his domain, she got distracted by the insight into a different Gray the room offered. She drifted from certificate to certificate, medal to trophy. Until she spotted a small display set apart from everything else. Upon closer inspection, Kitty saw a number of photos of men in uniform standing in front of a fire station. Engines proudly displayed, shiny in the sunlight.

Her eyes moved over the photos before coming to rest on a framed photo and nametag. The kind usually sewn on uniforms. And the nametag read "M James". Picking up the frame, Kitty studied the photo. She could see a strong family resemblance. She wondered if it was Gray's father.

Returning the frame to its place, she spotted a newspaper article clipping that had been laminated. Reaching for it, she started to read. The tears were running freely down her face by the time she reached the end of the article. The heartbreaking story of a local firefighter who'd become a hero saving a tourist's life, only to lose his own in the process. A young father and husband.

Gray had been three when his father had gone into a burning building to rescue a tourist who'd passed out drunk with a cigarette in his mouth. While rescuing the inebriated visitor, he'd heard what he'd thought was banging coming from another room. Unloading the unconscious man on paramedics, he'd gone back to investigate the noise.

It was unclear exactly what had happened when Gray's father had returned to the building, but he'd not come out again. Teammates had found him dead in the hallway to the bedrooms. The case had never been solved. But Merrick James had been cited a hero and honoured as such. And now that boy had grown to be a man just like his father.

Kitty's heart ached for not only Gray but his mother too. She couldn't even begin to imagine how hard it must have been for his mom, but she'd made sure her boy had grown into a good man. A man his father could be proud of. More than ever, she needed to call her mom.

All it took to ease the band around her chest was hearing her mom's voice. Not wanting to share what she'd just discovered with her mom yet, Kitty had kept her conversation light. They'd talked about familiar things, things that brought comfort, so that by the time they rang off, she was feeling much better.

Undecided on what she wanted to do with the rest of her evening, Kitty decided to go see what the men were up to. Making her way down the hall, she heard an animated conversation going on in the living room. Not wanting to interrupt if it was work related, she stopped to listen for a moment.

What she heard left her ice cold and feeling ill. Like she'd been catapulted back to the night Gray had been trapped in tons of rubble and no one knew if he was dead or alive.

"You, better than most, know how incredibly lucky you were during that cave-in, bud," she heard Kyle say. "If another beam had failed instead of the one that did, that scene could have looked a whole lot worse."

"Yeah, I know it. But you also know it's part of the job, Ace."

"Sure, it's part of the job. But if the roles were reversed, you'd be on my back like a cheap suit to go speak to someone." The pause seemed interminable. Then, when Gray didn't speak, "Have you even spoken to Kitty about any of this yet?"

"No, Kyle. I haven't yet. I'm not sure I ever intend to. I'm not sure how she'll react."

"You kidding me? This is as much her life now as it is yours. Bud, you play this one so close to the chest it becomes a tiger by the tail situation. What happens when you let go?"

"At a guess, my friend, I'm going to say I'd be well and truly screwed."

"Well, it's your funeral." Kitty could almost hear Kyle shrugging. "I hope you know what you're doing."

For the second time in as many hours, Kitty felt tears stream down her face. Turning as quietly as possible, she headed back to the guest bedroom she'd been sleeping in to pack her bags. The decision she'd been grappling with since this whole emotional rollercoaster had started, it seemed, had been made.

They'd waited for nightfall. As the dark of night settled, they climbed out of the car. Having followed her to his house, they now knew their new target. They just needed to scout around the property to find a weakness, the best place to set a fire. If they couldn't get to him on the job, they'd catch him in his home – the place he'd feel most secure. The one place they knew his guard would be down. If the whore stayed, she'd be caught in the blaze. And she'd have no one to blame but herself. After everything they'd done for her.

CHAPTER 15

The game over, Kyle stretched. Gray knew how he felt. He was exhausted. And everything hurt, again. Out of the corner of his eye, he saw his friend look over at him.

"You need anything else, bud?"

"No, I'm good, thanks. I'm done for the night."

"Yeah. I'm pretty much done for the night too. In fact, I think I'm going to scoot on home. Get some shuteye."

"Sounds like a solid plan to me."

Calling out, Gray let Kitty know Kyle was leaving. She came into the living room to see him out. When she was done, she came back into the room. Without a word, she collected his medication and brought it to him with a glass of water.

Swallowing down the pills she'd handed him, Gray let his gaze roam over her face. He couldn't put a finger on it, but something seemed off. When she'd left him and Kyle earlier, she'd seemed fine. Now, she didn't. And he had no idea why.

"Everything all right there, honey? You seem quiet."

"Yes, everything's fine."

Her words and her body language were in direct contrast. She seemed to be holding her body very stiff. As if she were in pain. Reaching for her hand, he was taken aback when she snatched it from his grasp.

"Kitty?"

"Nothing's wrong."

"Then what was that all about?"

"What was what about?" Kitty asked. But Gray could see on her face she knew exactly what he was talking about.

"Seriously?" Gray waited for her to answer. When she didn't, he continued, "I can see something is wrong. Out with it."

He watched as she appeared to gather herself. His stomach sank. If she was having to prepare herself to say whatever she had to say, it couldn't bode well. She sat down on the coffee table, across from him. Giving him a long, measured look, Kitty took a deep breath. Letting it out slowly, she looked down and started to speak. Instantly, he regretted asking.

"I overheard the conversation you had with Kyle about the day you got trapped in the collapsed building. I didn't mean to, but I was coming down the passage, and you weren't speaking softly."

Gray's gut tightened further. He wasn't sure he wanted to hear any more. But he asked anyway.

"How much of it did you hear?"

"I think pretty much all of it." He watched as Kitty swallowed. Almost as if she were swallowing back tears. "I heard what Kyle said about how lucky you were. I mean, I realised that he probably wasn't telling me everything at the time. But…..." She faltered.

"But what, honey?"

"But I never realised, until this evening, just how much he held back from me."

Gray watched as Kitty fiddled with her nails. She didn't look at him. The silence stretched as he waited for her to continue.

"I'm not sure if I'm supposed to respond or…... I'm a bit at a loss here, honey."

She nodded. Sighed.

"Gray, why don't you intend talking to anyone about what happened?"

Not what he'd been expecting, Gray took a moment to reply. "I don't feel like I need to. When I'm ready to go back on active duty, I'll have to have a debriefing, and that will be sufficient."

Finally, she lifted her head and looked at him. At the look of devastation on her face, Gray inhaled sharply. It was as if all she was feeling was etched on her face for him to see.

"I'm sorry. I'm not as strong as you. From the moment Kyle arrived on my doorstep to tell me you'd been caught in that cave-in, it felt like my heart took up residence outside my body."

Gray watched as a tear trembled momentarily on her eyelashes before spilling over. He watched as it tracked down her face. His own heart clutched as he waited for her to continue.

"I lived fear like I have never known each moment I waited for news. And I wondered how others live this reality every single day of their lives. Parents, siblings, partners, spouses watching their loved one leave each day, wondering if it would be the last time. Fear constantly wrapped around your heart and lungs…..."

Kitty's breath hitched, and her words stumbled to a halt. Gray shuffled forward in his seat to offer her comfort. Shaking her head vehemently, she pulled back from him. Letting his hands fall to his lap, he waited for her to continue. There was much more there. He could see it in her eyes. The knowledge made him feel ill.

He had a suspicion he knew where this conversation was headed. And all he could do was pray he was wrong.

"It feels like you're living with a vice clamped around your chest. Squeezing, tighter and tighter. Making it so you can't draw a breath. You can't breathe, and you feel like you're about to lose your mind. All you want to do is scream for mercy, for relief, for something. Anything. To take this nightmare away."

"Kitty, I sorry–"

"I know this is your reality," she cut Gray off. "I know that this is something that all of you know is a possibility every time you go to work. And, academically, I did too. But nothing prepares you for when it does happen." The tears flowed faster. "I'm sorry, Gray. I don't think I can do this every day for the rest of my life. I thought I could. But tonight, I realised I can't. I'm sorry."

Knowing what she was saying, but wanting her to tell him he was wrong, Gray spoke.

"Kitty, what are you saying?"

"I'm saying, Gray, that I can't live this life. I'm done. I'm leaving you."

He'd seen it coming, and still it hurt like he'd been stabbed in the chest with a hot poker. He'd hoped he was wrong, but he'd known. He'd seen it in her eyes. But god, it hurt to hear her say the words.

"Baby, please don't do this. Let's go talk to someone, together. Deal with it together. We can get past this."

Pain clear in her eyes, her voice little more than a whisper, Kitty replied, "That's just the thing, Gray. I don't want to. I don't want to live like this for the rest of my life. Fear my constant companion." Rising to her feet, she leaned down to place a soft kiss on his lips. "Goodbye, Gray. Take care of yourself."

Too stunned to react for a moment, she'd started to straighten when he reached out to stop her.

"Please. Don't. Don't make this any harder."

"Don't make it any harder? Seriously, Kitty?" The pain stabbed deeper. "You don't want me to make it harder for you? While you're the one slicing me open and leaving me bleeding on the floor?"

"I'm sorry," Kitty whispered as she backed away.

"Seriously?" Gray repeated. "That's all you have to say? You're sorry?"

"I have to go."

Turning his face away, not wanting to watch her walking out the door with his heart in her hands, Gray never said another word. Hearing the soft click of the door to the garage, he grabbed the glass on the table beside him. With a roar filled with all the pain and anger he was feeling, he threw it across the room. Watched it shatter against the opposite wall. Just like it felt his heart was doing.

***

Kitty was sure she'd made the right choice. But if that were the case, why did it hurt so much? She'd been drifting through the days in a haze. Almost as if she were living someone else's life. Nothing seemed as it should. It all felt wrong and out of sync. She didn't even know how much time had gone by. Days? Weeks?

When the buzzer had rung for the gate, she'd contemplated not answering. She'd been avoiding Morgan and Lee, but her friends were being persistent. It would only be a matter of time before they showed up at her door.

But when she went to answer, she was surprised to find Kyle on the other end.

"Open up, Kitty. I'd like to talk to you."

"Kyle, I'm not sure it's the best idea."

"I'm not leaving until we've spoken, Kitty."

Hanging her head, she sighed. "Fine. Come up."

Kitty waited by the door. But when she saw Kyle step off the lift, she almost lost her nerve. Very nearly closed the door. Stiffening her spine, she accepted the fact that he wouldn't be put off, and she'd only be delaying the inevitable.

As he reached her, she stepped aside. After he stepped past her, Kitty swung the door shut.

"Come through to the living room," she said as she headed down the passage. Going to stand in the middle of the room, she turned to Kyle. "What can I do for you, Kyle?"

For long moments, Kyle didn't answer. He merely studied her. As the silence stretched, Kitty shifted uncomfortably under his scrutiny. And finally, when she could stand it no longer, she saw his shoulders drop. As if he'd been braced for something that hadn't come. Then he spoke.

"I came here intending to rip you a new one, but you look as bad as he does."

"I'm sorry?"

"I was so pissed off at you for hurting Gray and intended telling you just how pissed off. But looking at you, I haven't got it in me. You look as shell-shocked as he does."

Kitty didn't know how to answer that statement, so she didn't. She stood, waiting for Kyle to continue.

"The worst of it is, I can't say I was surprised. Or that I can really blame you. And that almost pisses me off more. I don't want to feel empathy for what you're going through. You hurt a good man, Kitty. And that's not cool."

"Please don't, Kyle. I know I hurt him." Swallowing down a lump, Kitty cleared her throat. "I didn't do it out of spite. I just cannot find a way to live that life. Worried each day might be the last I see him. Don't you see? It's best to walk away now, before it's too late."

"Before it's too late for...?"

"Before it's too late and I fall in love with him."

"I've got news for you, Kitty." Kyle took her by the shoulders and guided her over to a mirror hanging on the wall. "Take a really good, hard look in that mirror."

Confused, Kitty looked at Kyle through the mirror. "I don't follow."

"When did you last have a good night's sleep, Kitty?"

Kyle's question caught her off guard. *Good question. When had she last had a good night's sleep?* Thinking back, Kitty was shocked to realise it had been before she'd broken things off with Gray.

"Since before I broke up with Gray," Kitty replied reluctantly.

"Yeah, that's what I thought." Kyle shook his head. "You silly woman. It's plain as day for anyone who's looking. It's already too late." All Kitty could do was stare at Kyle, speechlessly. He stared back before saying, "I'll see myself out."

She stood there for a long time after she heard him leave, too stunned to move. Eventually, not sure how much time had passed, Kitty made her way over to the sofa and fell onto it, her mind in turmoil.

Walking away from Gray had *seemed* like the smart thing to do at the time. Emotions were high and things had been said in the passion of the argument. Things she wasn't proud to own up to. But she hadn't seen her way clear to living like that every day for the rest of her life. Fearing for his life *every time* he left for work.

Panic and fear had been her constant companions from the moment Kyle had told her Gray was trapped in a burning building. Uncomfortable companions at best. To be fair, he didn't fight fires regularly anymore. But his job still held that element of risk.

It had been her reality for the seemingly unending hours she'd waited for them to dig him out of that collapsed building. The agonising uncertainty – was he still alive under all that rubble? Would she ever get to see his heart-stopping smile? Or hear that husky voice that set all her nerve ends tingling?

It had all been too much for her to deal with so, in the heat of the moment, it had seemed smart to walk away. Leaving the relationship before she got in too deep would save so much heartache in the long run. Not having to live with that daily doubt.

Apparently, though, the last laugh was on her. Standing in front of the mirror with Kyle at her shoulder, she'd realised, with the force of a sledgehammer, she was already in too deep. Way too deep. She'd fallen in love with Gray.

Yet Kitty couldn't quite put her finger on the precise moment she'd tipped over that edge. Somewhere along the way, he'd had crept into her heart. Softly, slowly, she'd fallen. The landing so gentle she hadn't even felt it.

Now, she was trapped in an unending cycle of emotion. Like a pendulum, emotion swung wildly between certainty and doubt. At the time, she'd been convinced she was doing the right thing for herself. Now, it seemed, she might have done just the opposite.

In hindsight, had she walked away from what could be potentially the best thing in her life? Had she made the biggest mistake of her life, thinking she was protecting herself? She just didn't know anymore. She was so tired of the constant see-saw of emotion. Thoroughly sick of herself, if she were being completely honest.

She had no idea what the hell she was going to do. Just knew she needed to do something.

Oh love, please forgive us. We didn't mean all the things we said. We were just so angry and couldn't think clearly. We understand now. It was his doing all along. He's tricked you with his smooth lies into believing that he's the right one. But it's okay. We'll fix it, you'll see.

CHAPTER 16

Plans to reopen Decadence were well underway. Kitty had thrown herself into the task of getting her business back up and running as a means of coping with the loneliness. The days were busy and kept the emptiness she felt at bay. But nights were always the hardest. When there was nothing to distract her, and her thoughts would constantly return to her time together with Gray.

The unexpected ringing of her cell phone had Kitty jumping in the silence of the apartment. Looking at the display on her cell, she was surprised to see Gray's number. Since she'd walked out of his house months ago, she hadn't heard a word from him. Pressing the green phone to connect, she answered.

"Hi Gray."

"Hey Kitty. I, ah– I know you asked me not to call, but I just wanted to see how you're doing." He was quiet for a moment. "Ah, screw it. If I'm being completely honest, I phoned because I need to hear your voice. I miss you," he replied in what she thought of as his melted chocolate voice.

Closing her eyes, she let the pain wash through her. She

knew how he felt. Missed him so badly it ached. So many times, she'd reached for her phone to call him only to remember she'd couldn't. And she had no one to blame but herself. She'd been the one to cut all ties, the one to walk away.

Over the past weeks, she'd gone back and forth over her decision. Had she made the right one? Her head told her she had. Living with the fear of his job every day wasn't something she was sure she could or wanted to live with.

Her heart told her she was a fool. Men like Gray didn't come along often. He cared about her and wasn't afraid to show her, or the world, that he did. Had she made the biggest mistake of her life by telling him goodbye?

"I'm sorry, Kitty. You asked me to leave you be. I should have honoured that. I won't bother you again."

She'd hurt him by not speaking while silently rehashing her decision – she could hear it clearly in his voice.

"No, no. It's fine. Sorry, I was distracted for a second. I'm doing okay. How about you? How's the leg doing?"

"Doing better, thanks. That's not to say I don't still have problems with it. But physio is definitely helping. I'm back at work now. I've been benched for another couple months. But at least I've got things to keep my mind occupied."

"I'm glad you're doing better. How's the case going?"

"Getting there. Kyle's been helping me sift through reports and evidence, and we're making some really good progress."

"That's great news, Gray. I know this case has been weighing on you."

"Yeah, but I'm finally starting to feel more optimistic about it. Something's been niggling at me since this whole torching spree started, and I've had an idea that I want to look into. If I'm right, then it's going to crack this thing wide open."

"That's really good news, Gray." Kitty knew she was repeating herself, but she felt so awkward. She didn't know what else to say. It wasn't like she had the right to ask him all the things that she wanted to. That right had been lost the moment she'd ended their relationship. "Well, I know you're busy, so I'll let you get back to it."

A couple heartbeats of silence passed. Then, "Yeah, I should probably get back to it. I'm sorry if I interrupted anything. It's just— I miss you, honey."

Gray's softly spoken words had tears filling Kitty's eyes. He was a strong, confident man who knew what he wanted from life, and she'd hurt him because she was a coward. Listening to Gray's words, hearing the emotion in them, she realised just how much she'd hurt him. She'd taken what he'd given her and thrown it back in his face. But damn it, she was hurting too.

Emotion slammed into her with the force of an ocean riptide, leaving her shaken. She hurt because she loved him. She'd panicked when he'd been trapped, injured. That things could have turned out very differently had her running scared. She'd run away rather than risk her heart. *Oh god, what had she done? She'd thrown away the opportunity to find a love like her parents had shared in all the years of their marriage. She'd had it in her grasp, and she'd wasted the chance.* The thoughts tumbled through her mind.

Maybe all wasn't lost. After all, Gray had reached out, hadn't he? The ball was squarely in her court. Did she have the courage to pick it up and engage in the game? If she wanted to see where this could go, she needed to man up.

A soft smile came to her face, and she replied, "I miss you too. I'm glad you called."

Gray inhaled harshly. The sound of it carried clearly over the line. "Honey—"

"There's so much I want to say to you," Kitty cut him off. "Things that need to be said face-to-face."

"I'm not sure I can wait that long. In fact, I know I don't want to wait. Talk to me, honey. Tell me what's on your mind."

"Well, for starters, I need to tell you how sorry I am."

"What are you sorry for, Kitty?"

"For walking out on you when you needed me. For throwing away what we were building because I was scared."

"Damn it! I wish I could come over. You're right, this is a conversation best had in person," Gray said. "I'm not going to lie, it hurt like hell, you walking out on me. But I get why you did it. If it helps, this thing between us scares me too. But I'm willing to take the chance if you are." A beat of silence. "So, are you?"

Without hesitation Kitty replied, "Yes, I am."

"I need to get back to work, but I'd like to come over when my shift ends. Would that be okay?"

"I'd like that."

"I really have missed you, honey. I've missed talking to you, spending time with you. And I've definitely missed being with you," Gray said. Suddenly he asked, "Before I go, tell me Kitty, are you alone?"

The question seemed a bit odd, but she answered him. "No, my mom's here with me. She popped in for a visit. Why?"

Instead of a direct answer, he answered her question with a question of his own. "Will you do something for me, Kitty?"

"Um, sure. What's up?

"Can you get away from your mom for a few minutes?"

"I– probably. Why, what have you got in mind?"

"Go into your bedroom and close the door. And Kitty?"

"Yes?"

"Make sure you can't be disturbed."

His voice had gone husky, putting her hormones on high alert.

"Okay, hang on a sec."

Gray heard her close the bedroom door as he locked himself in the bathroom. He was so hard for her he ached. And all it took was hearing her voice on the phone. He'd never live it down if Kyle saw him like this. He didn't want to take care of it alone, but there was no helping that now, so a bout of hot phone sex would have to do.

A rather inspired thought, if he should say so himself. He had missed her in the months they'd been apart. He'd tried his best to honour her wish to cut all ties. But as the days had turned to weeks, the ache had grown. It had been as if he was missing an important part of himself – like his heart. Today, his control had snapped, and he'd given in to the desire to hear her voice. And now, here they were.

"You still there?"

"Yes." Her breathless response made him smile.

"Get naked for me, baby."

"Um– Gray..."

"Please, Kitty, do it for me?"

The rustling of her clothing was the only answer he got, making him smile. He couldn't believe his luck. It seemed she was game.

"I'm naked, Gray."

Biting back a growl, he asked, "Tell me, Kitty, are you wet for me?"

Even though he couldn't see her, he knew, without a doubt, she was worrying that pouty bottom lip of hers in the way she knew drove him crazy.

"Yes," came the whispered reply.

Groaning, he lowered the zipper on his uniform pants. He was so hard it felt like he was going to burst through the teeth on the damn thing if he didn't. Lowering the pants and his boxer briefs just enough to take himself in hand, he said, "Touch yourself, baby. Rub your clit for me. Let me hear you pleasure yourself. Close your eyes and pretend it's me touching you."

He heard her draw a swift breath in, could almost feel her response to his words. Closing his eyes, he called to mind the image of her naked and aroused, stroking up and down his length with those soft hands of hers. What he wouldn't do to be there with her now. To be the one touching her. He'd give almost anything to be there watching her come undone for him. She was spectacular when she lit up for him.

"Honey, slip your fingers into that tight little sheath of yours," he groaned. "Let me hear you, baby."

"Oh God, I'm so wet for you, Gray. Just listening to you makes me hot. Are you touching yourself too? That would make me so much hotter."

"Yeah, baby, I'm touching myself. Just thinking of you makes me hard. Thinking of you touching yourself? Knowing I'm the one you're thinking of while you pleasure yourself? It makes me want to come out of my skin. I'm going to come so hard for you, baby. Want you with me when I do, honey. Tell me you're close."

"Yes. Oh god, yes."

He heard the hitch in her breath that told him she was at breaking point. Tightening his fist, he stroked himself faster, feeling it build.

"Gray...," he heard her moan his name, drawing it out, and he knew she'd reached that point.

"That's it, honey, give to me. Let me hear you. Come for me, baby."

"So good. Oh god, I'm coming, Gray."

She let out a breathless moan that seemed to go on forever. It tipped him over the edge and into his own orgasm. Letting out a groan of his own, he rested his head against the closed door.

"Damn, Kitty!"

On a breathless laugh, she replied, "Yeah, damn!"

After they'd taken a moment to calm their breathing and put their clothes back in order, Gray eventually said, "I'm sorry, honey. I hate to end it there, but I've got to go." Regret filled his voice, and he hoped she heard it.

"It's all right. I know you're busy. Thank you for calling me. I'm really glad you did."

"Er- Kitty?" he replied.

"Yes, Gray?

"I'll see you later then? I just don't know what time that'll be."

"I'd like that," she replied shyly. "Just give me a call when you're downstairs."

"Great. Thanks. Will do. Later then."

"Bye, Gray."

"Bye, baby." And after a moment's pause, "Kitty?"

"Yes?"

"Thank you."

When she replied, he could hear the smile in her voice. "Hmm, definitely my pleasure."

He laughed, and just before he hung up, he heard her doorbell ring through the line.

*W*here is it? It can't be gone. Think, think! Where did you last see it? Sweeping an irate arm across the desk, papers, photos, and assorted items went flying, landing on the floor haphazardly. Unmindfully stepping on the jumble of things on the floor, pulling on their hair, they seethed. Where did you put it? Think, think! Knocking their fists against their head, they rocked back and forth, repeating the words like a mantra.

They couldn't wait anymore. They only hoped she was ready. They'd had to step up the plan. They'd lost it, and now he'd probably figure it out. They couldn't stay. But they couldn't leave without her. Even though she wasn't with the hotshot fire investigator anymore, they couldn't chance it. She belonged to them, not him. OURS! Hang on, we're coming, love. Just wait for us.

---

*W*ho on earth could be at the gate? Surely it couldn't already be Gray. She hadn't yet heard from him. And she wasn't expecting any other company tonight. Her mom had popped in to see her, and they'd ended up having a girly night in. Chinese, wine, and girl talk had seemed exactly what she'd needed to distract her.

Getting off her bed, Kitty pulled her clothes straight. She couldn't help but smile thinking about the phone call she and Gray had just shared. Letting herself out of her room, she saw her mom coming out of the kitchen.

"It's all right, Mom, I've got it."

"You expecting company, Pussycat?"

"No, not yet. I wonder who it could possibly be." A frown

creased her forehead. "I'm not expecting anyone right now. Maybe it's one of the girls."

"You want me to open for you?" her mom asked.

"No, it's ok. I've got it," Kitty replied, heading for the phone receiver for the gate lock. "Hello?"

"Hi, Kitty. Hi. Um– it's Arch... Archie. Can I... can I come and speak to you? Please?"

Hearing Archie's voice, her heart sank. He was definitely the last person she wanted to speak to. She didn't have the emotional strength to deal with him. But she didn't have it in her to send him away either. Sighing, she hit the release on the gate.

"Sure, Archie. Come on up." Sighing again, she hung up, not looking forward to the visit.

Opening the front door, she waited for the lift. Looking toward the elevator doors, all Kitty could see was an enormous bunch of tulips and legs get out on her floor. They were absolutely spectacular. Some deep, vibrant colours of reds, oranges, pinks, and purples, and the pure white of untouched snow. Simply gorgeous.

The huge bunch of flowers and accompanying legs stopped in front of her. Holding the flowers out to her, Archie popped his head out from behind them. Blushing a bright red, he ducked his head when he saw her looking at him instead of the bright blooms.

"Hey, Kitty, Hi."

"Hey, Archie."

"These are– um, these are for you."

"They're lovely. Thank you." Standing back, Kitty invited him in.

Directing him down the passage, she told him to go on ahead to the living room. Her mom got to her feet as they came into the room.

"Oh, those are lovely. Let me get them into some water for you, Pussycat."

"Mom, I don't know if you remember him, but this is Archie Durwood. We were at school together."

"Yes, I remember you going to school with an Archie. Hello, dear. Nice to see you again."

"Evening, ma'am," Archie lisped. His colour deepening again.

"If you'll both excuse me, I'll go pop these into some water."

"Thanks, Mom."

Giving her a loving smile, her mother left the room.

"Have a seat, Archie. Can I get you anything to drink?"

"Um, no– no, that's not necessary. Thank you."

"So, what brings you by this evening?"

"I, er– I..." Archie grimaced.

Kitty recognised it as a sure sign of agitation. He always pulled that face when he was upset about something or couldn't find the words to express himself. As he went to try again, the gate buzzer sounded once more.

"I'll get it," she heard her mom call.

"Thanks, Mom." Smiling at him, Kitty continued, "Sorry, Archie. You were saying?"

Voices coming down the hall warned of more visitors. Looking toward the door, she saw Lee with her mother.

"Hey, Lee. What are you doing here?"

"Hey, babes. I need to chat to you about something, but I see you've already got company."

"No problem. Why don't you visit with Mom for a bit while I talk to Archie? We can chat after."

"Yeah, sure thing. I'll do that."

"Again, my apologies, Archie. It seems a little crazy here all of a sudden. Go ahead."

"Kit– Kitty, I, er... I wanted to apologise for my behaviour in the bakery the last time I saw you. I– I behaved appallingly. It– it wasn't– um, wasn't right. And I'm sorry. Truly sorry. Please forgive me?"

"Thank you, Archie. Apology accepted. Just as long as you know that we can never be more than friends."

"Is it– er, is it because of the fire guy?"

"Yes, Grayson is in my life. But no, Archie, you and I were never going to be more than friends. I like you, just not in a romantic kind of way."

"You and Gray back together?" Lee spoke from the doorway.

"Yes. I was going to tell you about it now when we chatted."

Lee didn't look pleased to hear the news she and Gray were back together. Then again, neither did Archie. Kitty sighed. She needed coffee. Or better yet, she needed a stiff drink to deal with all the emotions in the room.

Why? What did we ever do to you that you won't love us? Jealousy seethed through their system, and the madness took a deeper hold. You ungrateful whore! How can you still pick him over us? He doesn't have the first clue how to love you right. After all we've done for you, this is how you thank me? Enough! This ends now.

CHAPTER 17

R ubbing his hands tiredly over his face, Gray was ready to beat the hell out of something. He was sick of going over the same evidence, knowing he was missing something vital. It was there; he knew it was there. But what was it? For the millionth time, he mentally ran through the evidence again. In the back of his mind, he knew something about the pattern was familiar. He just couldn't put his finger on it. *What the hell am I missing? What is it that's hiding in plain sight?*

At the knock on his door, he turned. Smiling, he waved Kyle in.

"Kyle. Come in, come in. Save me from myself."

Laughing, Kyle opened the door wider and stepped into the room. "What's got your knickers in a twist, college boy?" he quipped.

Snorting, Gray motioned for Kyle to take a seat and took the chair next to him instead of going around to the other side of his desk.

"I'm missing something. Something important. It's there,

I know it is, but I keep missing it. Something about this whole setup seems *so* familiar, but I just can't pin it down."

"Want to go down to the gym and beat the hell out of each other, and see if that doesn't clear the cobwebs, old man?"

"I'll show you old man," he growled.

Kyle laughed again, knowing how much it irked Gray that he called him old man even though he was only five years older. Heading for the door, he stepped back for Gray to pass him. "Age before beauty, sir," he joked.

Ducking as he saw Gray swing at him, he took off down the passage, laughing as he went. "Last one in the ring buys the drinks."

Stepping into the ring with Kyle, he let go of all the thoughts crowding his head. For all his joking and pranks, Kyle was a good friend. He knew it always helped him to clear his head and change his focus to get into the ring, spar a couple of rounds. He could come back to a case with a refreshed mind. Clear thought process. A fresh eye. It helped him to see it from a different angle.

Hopefully, it would work equally as well this time, because he knew, without a doubt, that the answer to solving this case was right there in front of him. If he could just see it. He needed to go over the analysis report the lab had sent back, again, and look over the evidence with a fresh perspective. But for now, he had to focus on not getting his head knocked from his shoulders.

"Yo, old man. You ready to rumble, or are you going to stand there gathering wool all day?"

Knocking his gloves together and then against Kyle's, he threw himself into the physical release of trading punches.

"Just remember, loser buys the drinks, pipsqueak."

"Oh-ho, it's like that, huh? Bring it, old man. Let's dance."

After trading blows for over an hour, the two of them threw themselves down on the benches in the steam room.

"So how does it feel to get your ass whipped by an old man, pretty boy?"

Snorting out a laugh, Kyle quipped, "Don't let it go to your head, you old geezer. I let you win. Didn't want you crying foul for beating on an old man."

Flipping him the bird, Gray laughed. Changing the topic, they chatted about this and that as they sweated the ache out of their tired muscles.

Finally making their way to the showers, Kyle asked, "Listen, bud, you want me to come up to the office with you, let you run some stuff by me? Maybe between the two of us, we can figure out what it is you're missing."

"Thanks, man, that'd be cool. An extra set of eyes and ears might be exactly what I need."

"Sonofabitch! I can't believe it's taken me so long to see it. I knew I was missing something," Gray exclaimed in frustration. "I should have seen this sooner."

Rubbing his eyes tiredly, Kyle asked, "What did you find?"

Pointing at the evidence bags lying on the desk in front of them, he replied, "I knew there was something familiar about the pattern presenting in the fires. I just couldn't put my finger on it. Take a look at these photos of the scene together with the evidence I've collected from each fire site. What do you see?"

Stepping closer to the forensic bags containing the evidence and the lab analysis reports, Kyle reached out a hand to snag one of the reports. He took his time reading over each report, went over the evidence laid out, sifted through the photos of each site, and finally, he turned to read through each of Gray's reports related to each fire they'd attended in Kloof Street.

Gray silently watched him, waiting for him to get through all of it, to see what he made of it. Impatient to see if Kyle would see what he'd seen. Or was he grasping at straws here in an effort to solve this case? But when he saw him go back to a specific evidence bag, Gray knew he was right.

"Hot damn! You've got to be jacking me." Kyle's eyebrows looked like they were going to climb right into his hairline. "I was new on the team, a rookie at the time. This one was lighting them up all over the peninsula. It seems they were focused on some woman. Thought she was the one for them. She had business problems, and they seemed to think that burning the Cape down was a good way to 'make them go away' while getting her attention at the same time. Letting her see they 'were looking out for their woman'. Total fuckin' whackjob."

"I can't believe I missed it. It's been right in front of me this whole time. I knew I recognised the work, the pattern. It's only when I found that" — he indicated the item in the evidence bag Kyle held in his hand — "the pieces started to fall into place."

"Why would you have thought of them? Last I heard, this crazy mother was still locked up. And they should be there a good long while after all the crazy crap they got up to last time. Could it possibly be a copycat?"

"I have no idea. It's possible, because last I heard, too, they were still locked up."

"Ok, so, what do we do next? Where to from here, bud?"

Reining in his emotions, Gray took a deep breath and considered his options.

"Let's have a look at their profile on the database, see what we're dealing with. Refresh our memory some more. It's been a while since I last dealt with this crazy. Let's get these details out on the wire. Then I'm going to hunt them down. When I find their sorry ass, I'm going to make sure they're locked up for good this time. We're just lucky this nutter hasn't killed anybody yet. We've got to get them off the streets before our luck runs out."

Seating himself at his desk, Kyle hanging over his shoulder, Gray logged into the national database. Typing in the name and information he had, he waited for the profile to load. When it did, he felt his whole body go ice cold. He knew that face and realised he'd seen it recently. Very, very recently.

"*Fuck!*" Launching himself out of his chair, he raced for the door. "Come on, Ace. No time to lose. Let's get moving."

He was already reaching for his phone when he heard Kyle say, "I'll drive."

Kyle wore a bemused expression on his face since he probably had no idea what the hell had just happened – Gray didn't have time to explain himself. But one thing was for sure, it wasn't a good idea for him to be behind the wheel right then.

Sprinting for the stairs, Kyle on his heels, Gray said over his shoulder, "We need to get to Caledon Square. I need to speak to Captain Fourie there."

"Keys, bud. You're not driving in the state you're in. I'll drive; you do whatever you need to do."

Grayson bolted into the charge office at the Caledon Square Police Station in Cape Town's central business district, hoping Captain Fourie was still in. The officer on duty at the charge desk nodded a greeting and asked, "Can I help you, sir?"

Nodding in reply, Gray asked, "Captain Fourie still here, or has he gone home already?"

"No, sir, he's still in." Picking up a phone, he asked, "Who can I say is looking for him?"

"Tell him Gray James is here to see him."

Nodding again, the officer turned to the phone to place the call.

While waiting, he dialled a number on his phone, putting it to his ear. He'd tried three times already, but it kept going to voice mail.

After a brief conversation, the officer put the phone down, turning to Gray and Kyle.

"Come on through, Fire Marshal James. He's waiting for you in his office."

He heard his call go to voice mail yet again and tamped down the fear. Smiling his thanks as he heard the lock on the internal door snick, they walked through and down the passage to Captain Fourie's office. He put his phone back in his pocket, making a mental note to try again as soon as his meeting with the police captain was over.

His visit with Captain Fourie had done nothing to calm his fears. Instead, the sick knot in his stomach had just tightened. Voicing his fears that all was not well with Kitty as he hadn't been able to reach her for quite some time, which was very unlike her, the captain had suggested they go investigate, to set his mind at ease.

Dialling again, Gray was getting frantic. For the umpteenth time he was trying to get through to Kitty, and the phone just continued to ring, eventually going to voice mail. *Come on, come on, answer the phone, damn it. I know you're there. Just answer the phone, baby. Please answer the damn phone.* It went to voice mail yet again.

Kyle cast a glance over at him as the three men walked to the vehicle.

"You ok, bud?"

He just shook his head, pressing the phone to his ear as he tried again. Praying. He was plain scared out of his mind. He had a very bad feeling he knew why the phone was just ringing.

"Kyle, punch it. The phone keeps going to voice mail. Get me there, Ace. Before I lose my mind."

Not saying a word, Kyle did as he was told. Gray could see the concern on Kyle's face, since he was normally the calm, controlled one. He just didn't have it in him to put his friend's mind at ease. He was too freaked out himself. His gut told him all was not well. He could only pray he wasn't too late.

"Kitty, I've forgotten something in the car. I'll be back in a minute," Lee spoke from the passage. "Sure, no problem. I'm going to make some coffee. You want some?" Kitty asked.

"No, thanks. I'm good."

She studied Lee for a moment. She seemed a bit off, but eventually Kitty put it down to the stress of recent events. She was probably just projecting issues where there weren't any.

Turning to Archie, Kitty asked, "How about you, Archie? Some tea or coffee?"

"Are you sure, it's– ah, it's no problem? I can go, if you prefer?"

"Of course it's no problem. You're welcome to stay."

Elenore offered to make the beverages while Kitty entertained her guests. Archie excused himself to use the bathroom. Kitty had barely taken a seat when she heard what appeared to be a heated argument going on outside her front door. Spotting one silhouette through the patterned glass, she was confused as she'd definitely heard two voices.

"Who's there?" she called out as she made her way toward the door.

She saw the person turn to face the entry. Opening her front door, Kitty froze in horror. There was a gun pointed at her. The gun jerked, indicating for her to move back. Without conscious thought, she stumbled back inside before fear held her paralysed once more.

"Kitty, who's at the door?" Elenore asked, coming out of the kitchen.

Her mother's words shattered the immobility that the shock had induced. Turning to run, she screamed, "Run, Mom! Get to the bedroom."

"Don't you run from me, bitch!" she heard the incensed screech from behind her. Then the sound of a shot. Kitty kept expecting to feel the bite of the bullet, but it appeared to have been a warning shot. The burn she did feel, however, came from being brought to a sudden stop by her hair.

Unexpectedly propelled around by the force of the pull, she never saw the blow coming. Stumbling back a step, Kitty wiped a hand across her bleeding lip. Looking at her attacker, she felt a sear of anger.

"You b–"

Another shot rang out. The last thing Kitty heard was her mother scream out her name before everything went black.

His blood froze as he heard the shot and the scream that followed it. But nothing compared to the raw terror that ripped through him when he heard a second shot and then silence. Not a single sound.

"No!"

Gray didn't even realise it was him shouting as he ran. All he knew was he had to get to Kitty. If she died, it would be on him. If he'd figured all this out earlier, it wouldn't have come to this.

Kyle and Fourie close on his heels, they ran like the hounds of hell were chasing them. Not even bothering to call for the lift, they took the stairs two at a time. The sudden silence freaking Gray out, he snarled at Kyle, "Call it in and get an ambulance here."

Bursting onto the landing on her floor, he noticed Kitty's front door standing open. Cautiously approaching, he kept his ears peeled for any noise coming from the apartment. After what felt like an eternity, he finally reached the door. Slowly pushing it fully open, Gray stood clear of the opening. When no one fired at the space, he edged closer, peering around the corner to see a blood trail leading down the short hallway to the lounge.

He couldn't draw a breath. *God, please don't let me be too late. Don't let it end this way.*

Gray looked over his shoulder to see if Fourie had followed and saw the man draw his own weapon. Together they inched down the hallway in search of the woman who held Gray's heart in the palm of her tiny hand. At the entrance to the living room, he once more peeked around the corner to ensure he wasn't walking into a nasty surprise. He saw Kitty's mom sitting tied to one of the dining room chairs with a gag in her mouth as tears streamed down her face. Looking beyond her, his heart squeezed painfully. Lying on the lounge floor, also bound and gagged, Kitty's body jerked each time a boot landed a kick. He couldn't see who was doing the kicking.

Without warning, a voice screamed, "I did it all for you, you ungrateful whore! I did some of my finest work to help you get rid of all the competition around you. So that you could thrive and flourish. So you would be happy. And we could finally be together."

The voice stopped, as if waiting for Kitty to reply. When she lay, silent and unmoving, a particularly vicious kick landed in her abdomen. Gray could hear them breathing heavily.

The voice continued, "You said the bakery was your dream. That you had to focus on it, grow it, make it successful before you could even think of a relationship. I did it *all* for you. And how do you repay me? By whoring yourself with that fire investigator."

There was no reply, and Gray suddenly found himself praying. He was terrified. Kitty hadn't moved since he'd first spotted her lying there on the floor. Another unnerving silence followed. Fourie cocked his weapon, ready to fire. Holding it aloft, he stepped fully into the room, Gray at his heels.

At the quiet snick of the captain's weapon cocking, Lee turned her head. Her eyes locked on Gray's, and the first thing he noticed was the madness gleaming bright in the arsonist's eyes. The reports had said that Leyla Newman was delusional and should be treated in a mental facility. Prison was not the right place for her. Clearly, since her last stint, she'd finally fallen over the edge of delusion and straight into raving lunacy.

He watched as the gun Lee held in her hand started to lift in his direction, smiling in what appeared to be glee.

"Well, well. If it isn't Inspector Meddlesome himself."

"Drop it, Lee. It's over. This is Captain Fourie, and more police are on the way. You've got nowhere to go," Gray said quietly. "Don't make him shoot you."

An unholy rage fired in the woman's eyes.

"She's mine!" she screamed. "She's always been mine. But

you had to come along and interfere. Well, you can't have her. I'll see her dead before I let you have her."

Gray watched in horror as Lee swung the gun away from him back to Kitty. Without thought, he shouted, "No!" and heard another shot fired. He saw Lee's body jerk at the same time he heard Kyle come running down the hall toward him.

He watched in a daze as he saw Fourie step forward, kicking the gun that had fallen out of Lee's limp hand away. He saw the man check for a pulse. Obviously finding one, the man cuffed Lee with the handcuffs he pulled out of his pocket. Lurching toward Kitty, Gray hesitated. He was almost too scared to check her pulse. He didn't think he could bear it if she was dead.

Gray braced himself, pulling in a much needed breath before he reached out. His hand shaking, he placed two fingers on her carotid artery. He panicked for a second when he didn't feel anything. He pushed a little harder. There! He picked a beat. Faint, but there. He cut her bonds loose and dragged her blanket from the couch to cover her while they waited for the paramedics to arrive.

He glanced up when her mother dropped to her knees beside him, Kyle having obviously cut her loose. With a heart wrenching sob she dropped down opposite him. She put one hand over his holding Kitty's and the other under so she, too, was holding Kitty's hand. His free hand placed on top of Elenore's, they sat like that until help arrived.

***

Archie had been in the process of washing his hands when he heard the altercation in the hallway. Turning the tap off, he stood still for a moment to better hear what was going. When he heard the sound of a shot ring out, he went rigid with fear.

Cracking the door open in an attempt to see into the hallway, his heart almost stopped beating. He saw Kitty lying on the floor, unmoving, but couldn't see who her attacker was. Shock coursed through him when he saw a woman's hand reach down to grab a fist full of Kitty's hair before unceremoniously dragging her down the passage to the living room.

Closing the bathroom door as quietly as he could, Archie sat down on the closed toilet seat, rocking back and forth, as he tried to figure out what to do. After much deliberation, he decided the best thing to do was to attempt to sneak out of the apartment unseen. Once he was out, he would get help for Kitty.

Silently, he let himself out of the room and moved as stealthily as possible to the entrance of the living room. Stopping just short of the doorway, he paused to give his heartbeat a second to quieten down. It was beating so loudly he was surprised the occupants of the room couldn't hear it.

Finally gathering the courage to peek around the corner, he saw Kitty crumpled in a heap where she'd obviously been dropped. She wasn't moving; he couldn't see if she was even breathing.

Please God, don't let her be dead. I don't want to live if she's dead.

Cocking his head at a sound near the front door, he shrank back. Awkwardly, he shuffled backwards, quietly, into the kitchen to hide, keeping an eye as he did. He'd barely cleared the door when he saw the front door swing open and Gray move cautiously into the hallway.

Cowering in a corner of the kitchen, Archie's nerves stretched to breaking point with all the shouting and commotion. The noise ramped up his anxiety and was aggravated by the fact that he couldn't see into the living room. But he almost came out of his skin when more shots were fired. He hated not knowing what was going on.

For a time, there was silence, broken only by the sound of a woman weeping. Time seemed to slow as Archie waited in the kitchen. Rocking back and forth, his thoughts turned inward. Sitting in a bit of a trance-like state, he was startled by noise at the front door.

After a fierce internal debate, Archie crept towards the door of the kitchen. Carefully, he looked around the corner, trying to stay hidden, to see what the new noise was. Seeing a couple of paramedics with a gurney, he retreated.

Eventually, despite the fear, Archie couldn't take it anymore. As quietly as he'd slipped into the kitchen, he made his way back to the living room door. The shock of the scene unfolding in the living room had him gasping out loud. Shrinking back, he prayed that nobody had heard him.

Chancing another look, his eyes clung to Kitty's unmoving form lying on the floor. His heart beat hard and fast in his chest. His breathing rapid and painful. His Kitty couldn't be dead. He'd never have another chance to win her over. And the thought of that was just unbearable.

As the paramedics packed up and readied to transport Kitty, Archie retreated to the bathroom again. He would have a view of the passage from there. Closing the door until only a sliver remained, he watched as the gurney came into view. As they reached the front door, he heard one of the paramedics say, "We're losing her. Heartrate and blood pressure are dropping." No sooner were the words spoken when the heart monitor alarm sounded.

Dropping to the floor, Archie rocked himself. He heard nothing more, even as the paramedics fought to save her life. All he could comprehend was that his Kitty was gone. It was over. She would never be his. As tears tracked, unnoticed, down his face he planned his next move.

The confines of the cell were almost too much to bear. There had to be a way to break free. The thought of a lifetime stuck within such a small space was simply unacceptable. There was no way to exact revenge stuck in this hellhole either. And she would have her revenge!

CHAPTER 18

Pacing in the tiny waiting room as they waited for news on Kitty's condition, Gray finally understood what emotional hell she must have gone through when he'd been trapped. And then later at the hospital while she'd waited for news from the doctors.

What the hell was taking so long anyway? Surely, they should have heard something by now? He could feel the weight of Elenore's concerned gaze on him. He'd seen it in her eyes when his gaze had collided with hers at one point. He knew his behaviour appeared unstable, but he couldn't find it in him to reassure her he was fine.

Truth be told, if he told her he was fine, he'd be flat out lying. He wasn't. And he wouldn't be until he knew Kitty was going to be all right. There'd been so much blood on the floor. He hadn't known such a small body could bleed so damn much.

The door burst open, and Morgan flew into the room. Her frantic gaze searched until she spotted Elenore. Dashing over, she fell to her knees before the older woman.

"Oh god, Aunty Elenore, please tell me it isn't true? That none of it's true." Her tear drenched eyes clung to Elenore's.

The door opened again much slower this time. A lady Gray would guess to be around Kitty's mother's age entered the room. Walking over to Elenore too, she sat beside her and pulled her into a hug. Wrapping her arms around the newcomer, Elenore broke down. Holding her closer, the woman rubbed a delicate hand up and down Elenore's back.

Morgan, who had gotten to her feet, went over to where Gray stood watching them. Taking his hand in her smaller one, she gave it a gentle squeeze. Dropping his gaze to hers, he took in her pale face. As he watched, a tear tracked down her cheek. Then another.

He folded Morgan into his arms and tucked her head under his chin. Offered her what comfort he could as she cried. And all the while, it felt as if his heart was being ripped in two.

If this was anything like what Kitty had been feeling when he'd been trapped in that collapsed building, he understood it better. He could understand why she panicked, why she felt she couldn't live with the constant fear. It had been his shadow since he'd heard the sound of that first shot go off. Icy cold and insidious, it had his imagination working overtime.

Eventually, Morgan stepped back from his embrace.

"Sorry, Gray. I didn't mean to drip all over you."

Giving a snort of laughter, Gray replied, "No problem."

Turning to the woman with Elenore, Morgan made introductions.

"Mama, this is Grayson James. He's Kitty's beau." Turning back to Gray, she added, "Gray, this is my mother, Gwendoline Preston."

"Mrs Preston." Gray nodded at Morgan's mother.

"Please, call me Gwen. It's lovely to meet you, dear. I just wish it was under better circumstances."

The older ladies sat talking quietly as they waited for news on Kitty's condition. Morgan sat silently. Gray went back to his pacing. After what felt like an eternity, the doctor finally came to talk to Elenore.

"Mrs Spence, Gray." The doctor nodded at Morgan and her mother. "Kitty has been incredibly lucky. It was a bit touch and go for a while. Her blood pressure was dangerously low due to shock and blood loss. But thankfully, the bullet passed straight through, missing all major organs. She'll be fine. She just needs to heal."

"Oh, thank goodness," Elenore expressed. "Thank you, Dr Russo."

"Can we see her?" Gray asked.

"She's in recovery at the moment. But she'll be going up to the ward in a little while. I'll leave word with the nursing staff to expect you."

"Thanks, doc."

T he room reeked. It was starting to make Archie feel a little lightheaded as he inhaled the mix of chemical fumes in with each breath. He'd gone through Kitty's cleaning cupboard for anything he could find that might burn before liberally spreading it around her living room.

Now he was seated on the sofa, messaging his mother for the last time.

Mother, the key to my apartment is hidden in the purple pot plant by the welcome mat. Please take good care of my beloved plants. I love you.

Looking around the room, he finally made his decision.

Walking over to the curtains, he reached out and lit the barbeque lighter he'd found next to the candles in the cleaning cupboard. He watched, complete detached, as flames began to lick up the outer edge of the curtain.

When the flame burned, strong and bright, he moved over to the sofa he'd been sitting on. Repeating the same process as with the curtains, Archie watched as the sofa, too, began to smoulder then burn. One-by-one, he went around the room lighting the other chairs and soft furnishings, until the room filled with smoke.

The stench of the chemicals and burning fabrics of different kinds were starting to make him feel quite ill. Sinking to his knees on the carpet, beside the coffee table, Archie began to rock. It soothed him. Blanking his mind of all thought, he waited for the flames to consume him. So he could join his Kitty.

***

A meeting between the fire department and the police department had been held to go over the events that had taken place in Kitty's apartment that had ended in Archie torching both it and himself.

Captain Fourie had been placed in charge of the criminal investigation, while Gray had been assigned the task of assisting him and investigating the fire itself. They needed to confirm that it had, indeed, been Archie who had started it. And whether Lee had been working alone or if Archie had been helping her.

Now, standing before Archie's front door, his distraught mother waited with the key to let them in, Gray felt on edge. He didn't know what would be waiting for them on the inside, and it had him on high alert.

He'd requested that Kyle be allowed to assist him on this

one, and his friend stood at his back. He trusted the man with his life. Not to mention, he had a pretty sharp eye for detail too. Between them, they wouldn't miss a thing.

Feeling eyes on him, Gray looked up to seeing Fourie looking at him. An assessing gaze, as if he knew what was going through his thoughts in that moment.

"You ready, Gray?" Fourie asked.

"Yeah. About as ready as I'm ever going to be. Let's do this."

He watched Fourie turn to Archie's mother and ask her to open the door in a gentle voice. The captain was a tough, seasoned veteran of the police service, but it seemed he still had it in him to be gentle when required.

Gray felt his body brace as the front door swung open. Not sure what he'd been expecting, he relaxed a tiny bit when nothing untoward happened. Turning to Kyle, he spoke quietly.

"When we go in, stay sharp. We have no idea what's waiting for us on the inside. Be careful in there, yeah?"

"Got you," Kyle replied, equally as quietly.

Fourie and the two officers he'd brought with him entered, scouting the room as they went. Gray and Kyle waited to be given the go-ahead. Seeing Fourie nod, they stepped into a pristine, sparsely furnished living room. There was nothing in the room to indicate that it had been someone's home. It looked more like a budget motel room.

Following Fourie and his men down the hallway, the rest of the rooms yielded more of the same. Open doors had shown bland, impersonal rooms that looked like no one had ever lived there. With the exception of one door that was closed. And, upon closer inspection, was locked.

Once again, Gray saw Fourie turn to Archie's mother. A short discussion ensued, with the woman looking more and more agitated. He saw her shake her head repeatedly. From where he stood, he couldn't hear the quiet words Fourie spoke to the woman, but he saw her shoulders droop in defeat.

She turned and went back into the main bedroom, returning with a key in her hand. Giving Fourie a last imploring look, she inserted the key into the lock. Standing back for them to enter, fear was stamped all over her posture, hands wringing in clear agitation. And then Fourie opened the door.

Gray wasn't sure what he'd expected, but the room visible through the open door definitely wasn't it.

There were racks stuffed full of plants in bloom. Bright and bold colours, pastel and pale, all kinds of plants filled the shelves. He'd never seen so many plants outside of a plant nursery before. It all seemed a little strange. But it was only when he stepped into the room and took it in fully that his blood ran ice cold.

In a corner of the room stood a shrine. The walls were papered with hundreds of photos. And right in the middle, a huge canvas print photo, taking centre stage and highlighting the beauty of the subject.

The shrine and all the photos on the wall were all dedicated to Kitty. A timeline of his feelings for her over the years. Some of the photos dated as far back as their days at school together. Note cards peppered the walls, interspersed between the photos – notes of things he'd sent her, done for her, a record of all he'd done in his attempt to win her love.

One card stood out. It was dated the day Archie had set Kitty's apartment alight, with himself locked inside. He'd gone to her in a last-ditch effort to win her affections. He'd known, all along, that Lee was the arsonist, and he'd intended telling her it was her friend that had burnt her business to the ground. He'd never had the opportunity to tell her though, when Lee turned up unexpectedly and the chance was lost.

Archie had known everything about Lee. What she'd done, that she'd been in prison instead of "away on an extended business trip", all of it.. And he'd intended sharing his knowledge with Kitty.

Gray could feel all eyes on him as he stood trying to take it all in. He'd realised, from the way Kitty spoke, that Archie'd had a thing for her for years. He just hadn't realised quite how deep that "thing" had run. Squaring his shoulders, fighting the nausea in his gut, he indicated to Fourie he was good to go.

They'd systematically gone through the apartment. Bagging evidence, making notes, taking photos. Anything that seemed of interest, they'd bagged, tagged, and photographed. Finally, it seemed they were done. Gray couldn't wait to get out of the apartment and away from the shrine room, as he'd dubbed it.

Standing outside the apartment building, he attempted to gather his composure. Fourie came over to let him know they were on their way, and he'd be in touch to organise a meeting soon. Shaking the other man's hand, Gray said his goodbyes.

Turning to Kyle as the others left, he wiped a hand over his face. Blowing out a breath, he looked at his friend.

"Ace, we can never tell Kitty what we found in there. She's had more than enough to deal with. And I'm not sure this won't push her over the edge. She's been strong up until this point, but I'm not sure she's strong enough to take another blow this big."

"Yeah, I hear you, bud. Nobody needs to know about this."

"Thanks, man. I really appreciate it." Gray gave Kyle's shoulder a squeeze. "Thank god this day is done. Now let's get the hell away from this freak show and go get a drink."

CHAPTER 19

After a long three weeks in hospital, Kitty was finally going home. She couldn't wait. She'd been fortunate that the bullet Lee had fired at her had done minimal damage.

With her left arm still out of action for another couple weeks, and no apartment of her own, her mother had insisted she come home to recuperate. Much as she enjoyed her independence, she was actually looking forward to going home and letting her mother baby her for a while.

Gray, too, was being super attentive and sweet. He was spoiling her rotten, and she could get used this kind of treatment. If she didn't know any better, she could almost swear he felt guilty for what had happened to her.

If truth be told, she was still reeling with shock. She, Morgan, Archie, and Lee had all gone to school together. Morgan, Lee, and Kitty had been best of friends. Inseparable. How had none of them seen Lee's spiral into mental instability? How had they not known that she had lost her grasp on reality a long time ago? That she'd been a serial arsonist, responsible for an alarming amount of fires?

Things she hadn't really understood in the past made better sense now. When Lee had suddenly disappeared some years back without so much as a word, she and Morgan had been beside themselves with worry. Out of the blue, a couple of months later, Lee had phoned them from an unknown number to say she was travelling with the band she did promotion for.

While she promoted the band, Lee didn't generally travel with the band when they went on the road. She told them she'd been given the opportunity to travel with them on their world tour and had no idea when she'd be back. Kitty and Morgan had been perplexed at how things had played out back then. Now? Now it all made sense.

They hadn't seen how badly their friend had needed their help. But the thing that puzzled her the most was how Lee had been able to hide her descent into madness. Nobody had seen it coming. And then it had been too late.

Lee was now incarcerated, awaiting her trial. It would be some time before the case could be finalised. Yet, somehow, she'd managed to make a phone call to Kitty while she still lay in hospital, recovering. The woman had ranted, screaming abuse and threats of retribution, before Gray had taken the phone from her nerveless fingers and cut the call. He'd reported it to the prison authorities to be dealt with. But the interaction had left Kitty reeling.

Her doctor had suggested she talk to someone to deal with the trauma of being shot and then terrorised by a woman she had counted as family. Not forgetting that a man had committed suicide in her apartment, in a gruesome manner. When she'd agreed, Dr Russo had sent a colleague to see her in her private ward. She'd taken to the quietly spoken doctor, Dr Mason as she'd introduced herself, immediately. She knew, without a doubt, that Dr Mason was the right person to help her slay her demons and put her ordeal at Lee's hands to rest.

But, for now, she wanted to go home. She craved the familiarity of her mother's house.

I t had been a pleasant surprise when Gray had arrived with her mother to fetch her. She hadn't been expecting to see him until that evening. But it was so typical of Gray to be so thoughtful.

A wave of nostalgia hit Kitty as she walked into her childhood home. Yes, she'd been home to visit, but it was the first time she'd actually be staying at her mother's house since she'd left for college years ago. And the memories held within those beloved walls assailed her as she walked down the hall to her room.

Very little had changed. Other than the bed linens that had been updated in the years she'd been gone, the room remained pretty much the same. Almost as if time had stood still, waiting for her return one day. Feeling the burn of tears, Kitty blinked to hold them at bay. She moved slowly around the room, touching childhood knick-knacks that had meant so much to her then.

Hearing a sound at the door, she turned to find Gray leaning against the jamb. Without a word, he opened his arms to her. Moving into his body, Kitty soaked in the warmth of his embrace. Resting her head against his chest, she listened to the strong, steady beat of his heart beneath her ear. A feeling of a homecoming of a different kind settled over her. Like she belonged there.

"Your mom asked me to come call you. She apparently has a surprise for you."

She not only heard the words but felt them rumble through his chest.

"I'm not sure I'm up for any more surprises right this minute," Kitty replied.

"Yeah, I think you're going to really like this one though."

Pulling back so she could see his face, Kitty looked at him suspiciously.

"What have the two of you done?"

Laughing and shrugging at her, Gray simply said, "You'll have to go see, won't you?"

Kitty stepped completely out of the circle of his arms. Immediately, he missed the warmth of her soft curves pressed to his harder frame. He was still pretty shaken, realising that there could have been a completely different outcome. That he might very well have never gotten to hold her like that ever again.

Everything in him clenched at the thought of never holding her again. Or never getting to hear her laughter. Or simply never seeing her beautiful face again. A life without Kitty was unfathomable for Gray. He'd received a commendation from the city mayor for his part in solving the arson case involving Kitty's friend Lee, but none of it would have meant anything had he lost her in the process. More than ever, he understood that there wasn't life moving forward without her. It would merely be an existence, not a life.

Mentally shaking himself out of his morbid reverie, he held out a hand to her. "Come on, honey. Let's go see what's going on."

Giving him another look loaded with suspicion, Kitty

placed her smaller hand in his. Gray placed a gentle kiss on her forehead. Grinning down into her upturned face, he led her down the passage to the living room.

So focused on Gray was she, Kitty didn't notice her mother already waiting in the room. Nor did she notice the person standing beside her mother.

"Honey, I know you like looking at me," Gray teased. "But you might want to take a look around the room for a second."

Looking a little confused now, a frown creased Kitty's brow.

"Haha, wise guy." Gesturing to the room, without taking her eyes off him, she continued, "I've seen the room before. What I want to know is, what are you plotting?"

Putting both hands on her cheeks, Gray gently turned Kitty's head in her mother's direction.

"You sure you've seen everything to see in this room?"

Gray saw Kitty's gaze move over her mother and come to settle on the person beside her. He saw the exact moment her brain caught up with her eyesight. For a long moment, she stood as if she'd turned to stone. And then, with a cry of pure joy, Kitty launched herself at her brother.

"Phillip! Oh my god, what are you doing here?"

The other man laughed. "I heard via the grapevine you were getting into all sorts of trouble, so I came to see what was going on for myself."

Gray watched as she launched herself into her sibling's arms. He saw her grimace as her body made contact with her brother's, jostling her arm.

"Careful there, Pussycat. You don't want to do yourself another injury," Phillip cautioned before pulling her into a hug.

"I'm fine, but you're right. It's just I'm so excited to see you."

As Kitty finally stepped out of Phillip's embrace, she reached for Gray's hand.

"Have you met Gray yet?"

"Yes, I've had the pleasure. In fact, he collected me from the airport this morning before coming to fetch you from the hospital."

"Oh." Kitty's gaze moved between Gray and Phillip. "Exactly how long have the three of you been planning this?"

Gray, Phillip, and Elenore laughed at the disgruntled look on her face.

"A little more than a week," Gray replied. "We thought it would be a lovely treat for you to come home to."

"Sweetheart, I need to get going. There's a couple of things I need to get done. But I thought it would be nice if the four of us go out for dinner this evening. Do you think you'll be up for it?"

"Oh Gray, can't you stay?"

"I'm sorry, honey. I really do need to go. But it's only for a couple of hours. I'll be back before you know it. Besides, you and Phillip have a lot to catch up on."

Elenore, who'd been mostly silent up to this point, observed, "You need to take your meds and rest some too. You've had a busy morning so far, and I can see the lines of strain around your mouth. Even if you aren't willing to admit to it."

"I'm not a child, Mom," Kitty groused, a thoroughly disgruntled look on her face.

"I know, Pussycat," her mother soothed. "But you can't deny you're tired and uncomfortable, can you?"

Kitty sighed. Tenderly, Gray wrapped his arms around her. Placing a kiss on her temple, he stood with her in his embrace for long moments. Savouring her. Enjoying the familiar smell of her light, floral perfume.

"I'll be back before you know it."

Tilting her face up for a kiss, she nodded. Gray leaned down and complied with her request. The moment his lips touched hers, everything around them faded away. Nothing but the taste of her on his tongue, the sound of the breathy little noises she made when he kissed her, and the feel of her skin beneath his hands mattered.

Someone clearing their throat penetrated the fog of desire clouding Gray's mind. Smiling against Kitty's lips, he said, "I best be on my way."

"I'll see you out," Kitty replied, taking his hand in hers.

At the door, he gave her one last, lingering kiss. Gifting her that heart-stopping smile she loved, he let himself out, promising to see her later.

CHAPTER 20

Gray stood staring at the gorgeous ring in his hand. He had known for a while Kitty was the woman for him. He loved her with an all-consuming passion he'd never thought he'd find. But when she'd been shot and he'd been faced with the possibility of a lifetime without her, it had brought everything into sharp focus for him.

He realised he wanted marriage, children, the white-picket fence – all of it. And he wanted it with her.

While Kitty had been in hospital, Gray had taken Elenore to dinner one evening and asked for her blessing. After many of what he hoped were happy tears, Elenore had not only given her blessing but had told him about the ring her husband had given to her. One she'd worn with pride and love until that moment – long after he'd been gone.

Taking the ring off, she'd handed it to him and asked him if he would do both her and Kitty's father the great honour of carrying on the Spence family tradition. It was, after all, Kitty's inheritance anyway.

Moved beyond words, Gray had agreed to use the family

heirloom to propose to Kitty. The antique was an exquisite, emerald-cut diamond ring, steeped in history and clearly important to the family. And he felt flattered Elenore held him in high enough esteem to offer him the ring.

And here he was. The day had arrived. He would ask Kitty to marry him tonight, with her family and closest friends there to celebrate the happy moment with them. Or, at least, he hoped it would be a happy moment.

Gray paid the jeweller for cleaning the ring before heading for his car. He had booked at their favourite restaurant – the restaurant they'd gone to on their first date. While they would be taking care of all the catering, he had a last few things he needed to finalise to make it all as perfect as he could. Pulling out his phone, he called Morgan to confirm he was on his way to collect her.

Tucking his phone back in his pocket, he started the car. Anticipation hummed beneath his skin. He and Morgan were going shopping for what the woman had decreed the perfect engagement outfit. He'd seen firsthand the superb taste Kitty's friend had when it came to selecting clothes and so had roped her into the task.

Finally, everything was ready. Gray had dropped Morgan off so she could go get ready for the evening and was headed back to Elenore's house. He couldn't quite decide whether to be nervous or excited, as both emotions vied for first place.

For the millionth time, Gray patted his pocket to make sure the ring box was still there. The mere thought of losing the ring had him breaking out in a cold sweat. Reassured it was there, he blew out a harsh breath, telling himself to pull it together.

After pulling into the driveway, he parked the car. In a

few short hours, he would have the opportunity to ask the single most important question of his life. And he couldn't wait.

Climbing out of the vehicle, he saw Kitty standing in the open doorway at the front of the house. Waiting for him. It made him inordinately happy imagining a lifetime of such moments.

Taking in the goofy grin on Gray's face as he walked up the pathway to the front door, she wondered what had made him so happy. Whatever it was, happy was a good look on him. She knew that her shooting had shaken him to the core. It was a feeling she was intimately familiar with, having dealt with his own brush with death.

Her eyes lovingly roamed over him as he walked toward her. He was a beautiful man, both inside and out. Whatever she'd done to be blessed with his presence in her life, she was eternally grateful for it. She shuddered to imagine a life without him in it.

Kitty still had the occasional nightmare, dreaming of him leaving for work never to return to her. Along with her own ordeal, the fear was something she was working on overcoming. Despite thinking at one time that she couldn't live with the stress of Gray's job, she came to understand she simply couldn't live without him.

When he reached her, he stopped and stood, gazing deep into her eyes. As if he sought the answers to life's mysteries there. Returning his intense gaze, Kitty caught her breath at the love she saw in the depths of his emerald-green eyes. Eyes she would never tire of.

Oh, so slowly, Gray drew her into his embrace. Watching

her the entire time. Lowering his lips to hers, he took his time with the kiss. Almost as if he were trying to tell her without words what he was feeling.

Kitty got so lost in the kiss that her world shrunk down to nothing more than the two of them. The world around them simply disappeared. Sight, sound, sensation focused on him and the magic he was creating with his lips alone.

After what seemed like an eternity and no time at all, Gray eventually lifted his head. And Kitty was grateful to see he was equally as affected by the kiss they had just shared. Resting his forehead against hers, his lips barely touching hers, he gave her another of those intense looks. But it was what he said that took her breath away.

***

G ray had felt their kiss all the way down to his very soul.

Simple confirmation, unrequired but powerful nonetheless, that Kitty was the one. *His one.*

Resting his forehead against hers, lips barely touching hers, he looked deep into her eyes. Trying to convey all he was feeling but was unable to adequately express with words. The only words that would come were old as time, yet wholly fell short of encapsulating the depth and breadth of his feelings. But it was all he had to offer.

Cupping her cheeks, he stated simply, "I love you."

He heard and felt her indrawn breath. She closed her eyes for a moment, and when she reopened them, he saw it. Before she even said a word, her eyes told him.

"I love you too, Gray."

Music to his ears.

"Kits, are you planning on standing on the front doorstep all day? Or are you coming inside at some point?"

As she took a step back from him, Gray saw her roll her eyes.

"God, you're still a pain in my ever-loving ass, Phil. Don't you have anything better to do than harass me?"

Stepping to the side, she showed Gray to precede her down the passage.

Reaching out to take her hand, he turned to her.

"I want to make this evening special. It's not often that we both get to celebrate cheating death *and* having your brother here. So, I hope you don't mind, I asked Morgan to get you a little something for you to wear."

Excitement lit Kitty's eyes up.

"You shouldn't have. But thank you."

"She should be here soon to help you get dressed. Seeing you in the outfit will be all the thanks I need if it's anything like the little black number from our first date." Gray smiled fondly at the memory.

"If I know Morgs, I'm sure it will be. She has sublime taste in clothes."

Gray simply grinned in anticipation of the evening to come.

With his hand on the small of her back, Gray guided Kitty into the restaurant. Her mom and Phillip had gone ahead to get everything ready, and they were the last to arrive. The hostess smiled at them as they stepped up to her station.

"Good evening, Mr James, ma'am. Welcome back." Giving him a conspiratorial wink, she continued, "We've had a bit of a mix-up with the bookings this evening, and your table is no longer available. However, as such valued patrons, the manager has assigned the private dining room for your use to make up for the inconvenience."

"That's quite acceptable," Gray replied. "Thank you."

Out of the corner of his eye, he saw Kitty look first at the hostess and then at him. Giving her his best innocent smile, he guided her as they followed behind the woman.

The hostess opened the door to the dining room and stood to the side to allow them entry. As they stepped into the room, Kitty saw all the people who waited inside.

Turning to him with a confused look on her face, Kitty asked, "Gray, what's going on here? I thought this was a quiet family dinner this evening?"

"I was going to wait until you'd at least greeted everyone, but I should have known you'd be too impatient." Gray laughed.

He heard the door close quietly behind them.

***

T aking her hand, he gave her that beautiful Grayson smile that made everything in her melt.

"Baby, we've been through a rather difficult few weeks, the four of us. I've not brought it up because I know it upsets you to talk about it, but with all that happened, it made me understand just how precious life is. We don't know what tomorrow will bring and need to make the best of today. It also made me realise that I don't want to live one more day without you. I want you in my life. Every day."

So intent on the look on Gray's face was she, Kitty failed to notice the tears in her mom's eyes and the joy on her face. Or the man standing beside her. She completely missed Jeff taking her mother's hand in his, giving it a gentle squeeze.

Gray continued, "I had a whole speech prepared, but now that the moment is here, I can't remember a damn word. What I do remember is how you make me feel when you look at me – like I hold your whole world in my hands. When you smile at me like I am your whole world."

He paused, and she saw him swallow hard. But when he looked into her eyes, she *felt* like he *did* hold her whole world in his hands. He continued.

"Getting to know you, I've come to love so many things about you. I love your humour. I love that you're always smiling, spreading your own special brand of happiness to others around you. I love that you have such a gentle spirit but have the backbone and strength to take on bad times head-on, finding your way out on the other side. I love you, honey. You *are* my whole world. Will you marry me and complete my world?"

Reaching into his pocket, he took out a small, square jewellery box and opened it. Holding it out to her, Gray seemed to be holding his breath.

Kitty's eyes dropped from his own to the box he held out to her. Her eyes widened when she saw the ring nestled in the satin. Lifting tear-drenched eyes back to his, she could do nothing for a moment but nod.

Eventually she found her voice and whispered, "That was my gran's engagement ring. Dad gave it to Mom when they got married."

"I know, honey. Your mom gave it to me to give to you when I asked for her blessing."

Turning those tear-drenched eyes to her mom, all she could manage to say was, "Mom?"

"Pussycat, the day Daddy gave it to me was one of the best days of my life. And now it's your turn. May it bring you many years of happiness, just as it did me. More years than I had," her mother replied with a gentle smile on her lips and tears in her eyes.

"Well, honey, what's it going to be?"

Finally finding her voice, Kitty launched herself into

Gray's arms, laughing through the sobs. Despite the discomfort it caused her, she couldn't help herself. Peppering his face with kisses, all she said was, "Yes," over and over between the duelling emotions.

Gathering her close, Grayson kissed her until everything else faded into the background. The loss of the bakery, the fear of Lee's vicious attack, the pain of the betrayal, Archie's suicide and losing her home, all of it faded away.

It didn't mean that it had all *gone* away. It simply meant she'd finally found someone to quiet the inner demons. It meant that there, in his strong arms, she'd found peace. And love she knew would last well beyond this lifetime.

EPILOGUE

TWO YEARS LATER

ow long did it take to get test results anyway? she wondered, absentmindedly worrying at her bottom lip with her teeth. Surely the doctor should have been back by now. Unless the results were bad news. She hadn't even considered that.

Refusing to even entertain that thought, Kitty turned her thoughts to Decadence. She had left her new assistant manager in charge of the store while she went to her doctor's appointment. She missed Jazz terribly, now that the other woman was running the new branch of Decadence. But the replacement was working out well, and she was happy.

Finally, Kitty heard the door close behind her. Clasping her hands tightly together, she waited for the doctor to take her seat. She'd been feeling off-colour for a number of weeks. In the last couple of days, though, she'd begun to suspect she might be pregnant. All the signs pointed to it – the nausea, the tender breasts, the unexplained weight gain. And, most importantly, she was late.

She and Gray had been talking about it for a while, agreeing it was time for her to come off contraception. They were ready to start a family. The thought of a little boy blessed with his father's good looks and charm warmed her heart. She could picture him in her mind's eye. Winning the ladies over, just as his father did everywhere he went.

Kitty just hadn't thought it would happen so quickly. Despite them having made the decision to try, she wasn't sure how she felt now that the moment of truth was here. Sure, they'd decided the time was right, but that didn't mean she wasn't nervous as hell. She'd thought she would have more time to adjust to the idea of being pregnant. Of having a baby.

Dr Dias took a seat behind her desk, still reading papers in the file she held in her hands. After a couple of minutes, she looked up. Folding her hands over the file she placed on the desk in front of her, she gave Kitty a long look before she spoke. The nerves ramped up.

"Well Kitty, it seems your suspicions are correct." She smiled. "Congratulations. You are, indeed, pregnant. Nine weeks along it seems from the results."

Touching a hand to her midriff in wonder, Kitty took a moment to absorb the news. Excitement and apprehension rippled through her. There was no turning back now. She took a deep breath.

"Wow. I'm not sure what to say."

Looking a little puzzled, the doctor asked, "This baby is unplanned?"

Suddenly, that ripple of excitement burst to life. *Oh wow! This is really happening. I'm going to be a mom.*

Laughing in delight, Kitty replied, "No, not unplanned. It's just happened a whole lot sooner than we were expecting it to. Gray and I've only been trying for a short while." Her hand found its way back to her midriff, almost unconsciously.

"Then I guess that handsome husband of yours has some powerful swimmers," the doctor joked.

Laughing, Kitty asked, "So, Dr Dias, what happens now?"

Listening to the doctor with half an ear, Kitty's mind sifted through all the possible ways she could share the news with Gray. Should she wait a bit before she told him? Where should she tell him?

"And then we'll use an elephant dart to administer the epidural." No response. Not even so much as a blink. "Kitty, did you even hear a word I said?"

Kitty was pulled out of her thoughts by the amused exasperation in the doctor's tone. Blushing, she shook her head.

"Sorry, doc. I was so wrapped up in my own head. Forgive me."

"I know it can be a lot to take in." The doctor smiled kindly. "I'll give you some reading material you can go through that will give you the same information I was just telling you. You can digest it at your own pace."

"Thank you."

"Here's a prescription for some prenatal supplements I want you to take, and I'll need to see you again in a month's time. Now, let's get you set up for a scan so you can see your baby."

Standing, as the doctor rose from her seat, Kitty followed her out into the reception area to make the appointment. Suddenly, she couldn't wait to see her little bean.

"What date suits you for the follow-up appointment?"

Consulting her phone's calendar, Kitty gave the doctor a date. After a short conversation between the doctor and her receptionist, Dr Dias turned to her with an appointment card.

"I've had Nancy schedule your sonar for the same day as your appointment. That way we can see what's going on in there. Then follow it up with the physical exam and a consult."

"Thanks, Dr Dias. I'll see you then."

Feeling like she was walking on air, Kitty all but glided back to her car. A baby! Now she just had to plan a surprise to share the news with Gray. She wanted to do something fun. It was exciting news.

G lancing at his watch as his phone began to ring, Gray realised it was home time. Knowing he'd be going home to his wife – he still couldn't believe he'd been that lucky – was the best part of his day. He picked up his phone and checked the display before answering.

"Hi Beth. I hope you're calling with some good news."

"Indeed, I am, Gray. I've just heard back from the bank and thought I'd let you know right away."

"And? What did they say?"

"The mortgage has been approved. The house is yours. Congratulations. You're now the proud owner of a house."

"That's wonderful news, Beth!" Gray considered a moment and then asked, "Have you got time in your schedule this evening to meet up with us at the house? I'd like to take Kitty to see it."

"Yes, of course. Gosh, it's so exciting. I really hope she likes it."

Laughing, Gray replied, "Yeah, me too. Otherwise I've just bought a white elephant."

On a laugh of her own, Beth said, "How about six? Does that suit you?"

"Thanks, yes. Six is perfect."

"Excellent. I'll see you at six then."

"Yep, six. See you then."

Hanging up, Gray collected his things and headed for the door. He couldn't wait for Kitty to see the house. They'd been searching online for months, and when they found the listing for this house, they'd both agreed it would be perfect. In Kitty's case, it was sight unseen, but Gray had made an appointment with the estate agent to see it. He'd wanted to surprise his wife.

He'd invested the small insurance pay-out that had been ceded to him when his father died. Through the grief, Gray hadn't wanted to spend a cent of the money that would never be a replacement for the man he had adored. Now, the healthy growth of that investment had been ample to put a deposit down on a home he looked forward to sharing with the woman that meant everything to him.

On the drive home, he began to wonder if he'd done the right thing. Buying a house was a big commitment. What happened if Kitty only liked the house online and hated the real thing? They'd be stuck with a house she didn't like, and he'd feel like a prize putz for deciding without her. Unlikely she'd ever let him forget it either. Smiling wryly to himself, he acknowledged it was too late for thoughts like that. The deed was done. The best he could hope for was that she would love the real thing as much as the online images.

He knew his wife pretty well, sometimes better than she knew herself. He was confident he'd made the right choice. But only time would tell. In the meantime, he needed to decide where to take her to celebrate this milestone in their marriage. They had a handful of favourite restaurants, but he wanted tonight to be extra special.

Inspiration struck as he pulled into the driveway. Making a quick call to book reservations, he kept an eagle eye out for Kitty. Since her car was already parked in the garage, he knew she was home. He didn't want her to overhear his plans. He wanted tonight to be a night for surprises.

As he entered the kitchen from the adjoining double garage, Gray called out for Kitty. When he heard her answer from inside the house, he moved toward her voice. Meeting her in the passage, he pulled her in for a kiss, laying his lips on hers. He ran his tongue over that pillowy bottom lip that drove him crazy.

The kiss quickly burned hot as Kitty opened for him, her tongue twining with his, giving back all that he gave to her. Eventually pulling back, they took a second to catch their breaths.

"Hello, gorgeous."

"Hey yourself, handsome. How was your day?"

"Pretty good, actually. How was yours."

"About the same, I'd say."

She grinned up at him. Something in her tone made Gray pay closer attention to the expression on her face. It seemed his wife might just have news of her own. His curiosity piqued, he smiled back.

"Sounds interesting. What did you get up to?"

"Quite a bit actually, but I'll tell you in a minute. Before we start exchanging news about our day, what are we doing about dinner? I'm in the mood to go out for dinner this evening. Somewhere nice."

Chuckling to himself, Gray replied, "Yeah, that sounds like a good idea. I think I know just the place. I'll make the reservations. Okay if it's a surprise?"

Shrugging, Kitty asked, "What's the dress code?"

"Fairly formal."

"Got it. How much time do I have?"

Looking at his watch, he answered, "Is an hour enough time? I have a quick stop I need to make before dinner."

"It'll be close, but I can do it. Where are we going?"

"Another surprise."

For a second, it looked like she was going to launch into a game of twenty questions, but in the end, she simply nodded, then headed for the bedroom.

Despite asking where they were going several times, Gray wasn't telling. She didn't recognise the road they were travelling. It didn't lead to anyone she knew. So, it seemed she was going to have to be patient.

After a ten-minute drive, they pulled up to a security gate of a house she still didn't recognise. She didn't know anyone living in the beautiful, leafy suburb of Claremont. Gray consulted his phone, lowering his window at the same time. Then reached out and entered a code into the keypad beside the car. Slowly, the exquisitely crafted safety gates began to open.

"Why do you have the gate code for this house?"

"Wait and see," was all Gray would say.

Making a sound of irritation, Kitty sat back and took comfort in the fact that she had a secret of her own. She couldn't wait to see the look on his face when she told him about the baby at dinner. Putting her hand in her handbag, she reassured herself that the initial pregnancy test she'd taken was there.

When she'd begun to suspect she was pregnant, she'd taken a home pregnancy test. When that had come up positive, Kitty had made the appointment with the doctor to confirm the result. Almost unconsciously, her hand made its way to her still-flat stomach. Realising what she was doing, she snatched her hand away before she gave herself away. It would be so disappointing if Gray figured it out before she could tell him.

He stopped next to a car already parked in the driveway. Climbing out, he came around to her side and opened the door for her. He took her hand, making his way to the front door. Grinning at her, he gave a quick knock before opening it.

"Beth?" Gray called out.

"Who's Beth?" Kitty whispered, trying to see past him into the house.

She heard the clip-clop of high heels, and then, "Hi Gray. Come on in."

Kitty stiffened. Who was this woman? And how did she know her husband's name? But before she could ask, Gray turned to her and covered her eyes with his hand.

"Don't look until I tell you to," was all he said. She could hear the excitement in his voice.

He guided her briefly before telling her to stop and close her eyes.

"Are they closed?"

"Yes, they're closed," she replied.

"Promise?"

"Oh, for heaven's sake, you nutter. Yes, they're closed."

Gray laughed. Taking his hand away, he waited a beat before he murmured into her ear, "Open your eyes."

Kitty did as she was told. She was facing a wide panel of glass windows and sliding doors. But it was the view outside that absolutely took her breath away. Beyond the glass was, quite possibly, the most beautiful garden she'd ever seen. Lush foliage, a sumptuous expanse of emerald green grass, and a sparkling, impossibly blue swimming pool.

It was, however, the generous bank of flower beds bursting with a riot of colourful flowers of all kinds that demanded her attention. She caught her breath when she noticed that a large number of the blooms were carnations. Her father had grown carnations, and a flood of happy childhood memories overtook her. She could imagine a child of her own playing in a garden like this one.

"Oh, my goodness, Gray. What a stunning garden."

Turning to face him as he stood a little way behind her, the emptiness of the room caught her attention. Looking at Gray, she saw that smile she loved so much spread across his face.

"Welcome home, my love."

At first, she simply stared at him, unsure she'd heard him correctly.

"Wait- what?"

Taking her face in his hands, he laughed down at her.

"This is our house. I was looking for a gift to give you, to say thank you for the three years of love and joy you've brought into my life."

"So you bought me a house? Bit of a tough act to follow in the years to come, don't you think?"

Both Gray and the lady they'd met at the house laughed. Until that point, Kitty had completely forgotten they weren't alone. He turned his body toward the other woman.

"Beth, this is my wife, Kitty. Kitty, this is Beth. She's the estate agent that's been assisting me with the house."

"Hello, Kitty. It's lovely to finally meet you."

"Um- Hi, Beth. It's nice to meet you too."

"Shall we take a tour of the house then, now that Gray's wowed you with the back garden?"

Suddenly excited, Kitty grabbed Gray's hand. Nodding at Beth, she said, "Lead the way."

Beth took them through the house, pointing out features and points of interest as they went. For once, she was completely silent. Simply took in her surroundings as they went from room to room. Walking into one of the bedrooms, she'd known in an instant it would be the perfect room for a nursery.

After lingering in the room, imagining how it could be, she finally followed Gray and Beth into the master suite. Taking in the beauty of the main bedroom, she allowed her imagination free reign again. In her mind's eye, she could see the two of them spending summer evenings on the patio outside the French doors leading into that magnificent garden. Or winter evenings cuddled up in front of the fireplace in the corner of the room.

"Well, there you have it." Beth smiled at Kitty. "What do you think?"

"It's lovely. Just so much to take in," Kitty replied.

"Why don't you have another look around? When you're done, come find me, and we can finalise the paperwork."

"That sounds wonderful. Thank you."

With another smile, Beth left the room. Turning to Gray, Kitty took his hand.

"Come with me. I want to have another look at the second bedroom."

With her hand in his larger one, she walked to the other room. Leading him over to the window, she stopped there. Took the gorgeous expanse of garden in, marvelling at it yet again. Putting her handbag down on the windowsill, she rested her hand there a moment.

"I can't believe this beautiful house is ours. You were so clever at pulling this off so secretly."

"You're not upset, are you?" He looked worried.

"No, I'm not upset. It's too beautiful for me to be cross about it." Kitty smiled. Reaching into her bag, she felt around for the little stick. "I was wondering, what do you think about making this bedroom a nursery?"

"Yeah, I reckon it's a great room for a nursery," Gray said.

"When would we be able to move in, do you think?"

"Once the papers are all signed and squared away with

Beth, the house will be ours within a month. So probably a month to five weeks from now."

"Oh wonderful. That would give us enough time then."

Looking confused at her statement, Gray frowned. Joy, in its simplest form, washed through her. She held her hand out to him; tiny bits of the plastic stick peeked out either side of her hand.

"What's this?" he asked.

Turning her hand over, Kitty uncurled her fingers. The pregnancy test lay in her palm, display window up. Gray looked at it lying in her hand, and she saw the moment he realised what it was.

"Is it... Are you... Are we...?"

"Yes, the doctor confirmed it this morning. We're pregnant."

Laughing in sheer delight at the look on his face, she nodded. It felt so good to be sharing the news with him. To say the words out loud.

Gray gathered her up in a huge bear hug, swinging her around until they were both dizzy and laughing like children. Savouring the moment, Kitty tightened her arms around his neck, hugging him closer to her. She held her entire world within the circle of her arms. And she couldn't think of any place she'd rather be than right here, in this moment.

"Oh my god, I can't believe it's happening already." The smile on Gray's face was huge.

"I can't believe we've just bought a house," Kitty quipped in reply.

Lowering her to her feet, he took her face in his hands, looking deep into her eyes. Kitty swore she could see forever as she got lost in the love she saw there. She saw home and family and a lifetime of blessings with this incredible man by her side.

ACKNOWLEDGMENTS

As always, I could not have told Gray and Kitty's story without the love and support of my amazing tribe! I will be forever in their debt - my thanks to:

To my mom, my husband and my son for always believing in me and pushing me to never give up. Ryan, thank you for picking me up when I fall at the hurdle. Grant, as always, thank you for being my accountability partner. And Mama, thank you for the keeping the coffee coming, and doing the first read through. I appreciate it more than you know. Thank you to all of you for holding me accountable to my dreams, goals and deadlines. I love you.

To Kate Williams, Deon Smit, Jacques Laubscher, Brent Murtagh and Dorian Wheatley for your incredible insight into a dangerous job. For time so freely given and being willing to answer a myriad of questions. A million thank you's. Your expert insight has been invaluable, *and all errors are my own.*

To Candy Royer for the fabulous job you did editing this book and Marilize Roos for the wonderful job you did proofreading it. It was, once again, a pleasure and an honour working with you. I look forward to our next project together. Thank you!

And finally, to you the reader, a deep and heartfelt thank you. Your support means more than I can ever express. I hope you love Gray and Kitty as much as I do.

Much love, Dorothy xx

SNEAK PEAK

LOVE AT LAST

Have you met Adam and Willow yet? If not, here's a sneak peek into their story:

The moment she closed the door behind her, Willow realised something was wrong. Silence permeated the house, and the unexpectedness of it unsettled her. Since her friend, Meri, had moved in with her two months ago, the house was never quiet anymore. Meri loved music and always had it playing in some part of the house. Tonight though — nothing. Maybe she was overreacting, and Meri had just gone out. She really hoped that was the case.

"Meri? Are you home?"

More silence.

Willow moved farther into the house looking to see if she could find a note explaining the quiet; the lack of response. It was unlike Meri to go out without leaving a note or not to have told her in advance.

"Meri?" she called again as she moved into the living room. "Are you here, babes?"

Nothing.

"Meri, are you home?" she called once more, unease crawling its way along her spine.

Shrugging out of her jacket, she walked back to the

hallway to hang it up. A low, pain-filled moan caught her attention. The uneasiness ramped up. Moving through the hallway, she called once more, "Meri, are you in here? Are you okay, babes?"

Willow stopped to listen, trying to pinpoint exactly where the sound was coming from, hoping to hear it again so it would point her in the right direction. Then she heard the moan anew. Realising it was coming from the living room, she moved toward it. As she rounded the long sofa, she stopped in her tracks, unable to comprehend the sight before her. Meri lay on the ground, curled up on her side in a fetal position, clearly trying to protect the twins she was heavily pregnant with. She was severely beaten, lying in an ever-growing pool of blood beneath her hip. Icy panic flashed through Willow. That amount of blood couldn't mean anything good for Meri's pregnancy.

"Oh God, Meri." Willow dropped to her knees beside her friend. "Babes, can you hear me? Meri? Meri!"

Getting no response, Willow jumped to her feet. She raced back to the hallway to get her cell phone. Her hands shook so badly she misdialled three times before she finally managed to get through to the cell phone emergency line — 112.

"One-one-two, what is your emergency, please?"

Giving her name, Willow told the operator what the problem was as quickly and concisely as she could.

As the tears coursed down her face and her breath hitched, Willow could barely manage a whisper. "Please. She's pregnant, and . . . Oh God, there's just so much blood."

"Stay with me here, Ms Martin. I've dispatched an ambulance and the police. They're on their way to you as we speak," the operator soothed.

While staying on the line, Willow kept talking to Meri, trying to get her to respond. It seemed to Willow as if the blood was rapidly expanding. She was so far out of her depth that panic, icy and insidious, held her in a tight grip. By the time emergency services and police arrived, Willow's panic was full-fledged. She had never felt so alone in her life.

Standing to one side, so she was out of the way, she watched everything the paramedics did as they worked on her friend.

Just when Adam thought the day couldn't get crappier, it finally ended. He couldn't get away from the station quickly enough. He felt called to be a policeman since he was a little boy. It was all he remembered ever wanting to be. But days like today made him question the wisdom of his choice. Crime, in general, offended his moral code, but when it involved children, as today's case had, it was always difficult to deal with. It cut especially close to the bone now that he had a child of his own.

Giving thanks that he'd at least get to hold his infant daughter again, he headed to collect her from her day mother. He looked forward to some downtime to decompress, maybe relaxing on the couch with a cold one after he'd gotten Gracie settled for the night. A couple of blocks from home, his cell phone rang, interrupting the sounds of rock music flowing through the stereo as his daughter slept on in her car seat.

His partner ringing at this time of evening generally wasn't a good sign. It would seem likely that his crappy workday wasn't quite over yet. Biting back a sigh, he answered.

"Hey, Gav. What's up, bud?"

"Hey, man. Just got a call in from dispatch. One-one-two caught an assault, possibly attempted murder. I caught the case, but since I'm headed off on sick leave for my shoulder op in a couple days, Cap's decided he wants you to take over from me as the lead on this one. I'm almost at the scene now. I'll message you the address as soon as I get there. You can meet me there."

Mentally cursing, using every imaginative expletive he knew, Adam turned the car around, heading towards his parents' house instead of his own.

"Let me just drop Gracie off at my mom's. I'll be there as soon as I can."

He disconnected the call, dialled his mom, and ten minutes later dropped his sleeping baby off with his parents.

"Thanks, Mom. I appreciate it." Bending, Adam placed a gentle kiss on the older woman's cheek.

"You're welcome, my boy. Don't worry about Gracie. We'll keep her here tonight. Dad and I can drop her off at daycare in the morning. You just head straight home when you're done. A good night's rest will do you good. You're looking tired, my boy. You work too hard."

He thanked his mother again. After giving his daughter one last kiss on the head and hugging his mother goodbye, he headed to the address his partner had messaged him.

Pulling up to the house on a quiet street in an ordinarily tranquil neighbourhood, Adam absently noted the flashing lights. A few people stood around watching the commotion, huddling together and murmuring amongst themselves. It certainly was a sight out of the ordinary for them. Approaching the front door, he found it standing wide open, vehicles and people stood all over the driveway.

He stepped into the foyer and looked around for his partner. When he didn't spot Gavin, he called a uniformed officer over to inquire as to where to find him. She informed him the man was in the living room, pointing him in the right direction.

As he moved that way, he caught the sound of quiet weeping. Clearly distraught, they obviously needed someone with a gentle touch dealing with them tonight, but after the miserable day he'd had, it couldn't be him. He was all out. As he turned back to find the uniform he'd just spoken with, he caught a glimpse of a beautiful woman talking to a paramedic. He took a step closer to get a better look and felt somewhat dazed – a bit like he'd walked into a brick wall.

She was a tiny bundle of perfect. The policeman in him was ingrained. Even when admiring a good-looking woman, his well-trained eye assessed. He estimated she couldn't be more than five foot two or three. Although not overweight, she certainly had the voluptuous curves that a man craved to get his hands on. A mass of blonde waves tumbled down her back to just below her waist.

Pulling his gaze away from her, he started turning away. In his current mood, it was probably best to leave her to Gavin. He was good with people. He'd know what to say to make her feel at ease.

She chose that moment to unexpectedly turn her head, looking directly at him.

His heart clenched at the sight of her tear-drenched eyes, the colour of the deepest blue sapphires, still so beautiful despite the tears. Suddenly, he had an intense desire to haul her into his arms and comfort her, which made no sense at all.Adam had never had such a visceral reaction to anyone before. Changing his mind, Adam moved towards her. Those intense blue eyes followed his progress as he crossed the floor.

A sense of being watched penetrated the fog in Willow's brain. She turned her head to seek out the source and spotted a man standing in the doorway of her living room. Although she immediately noticed he was handsome, despite her grief, it was more than that. He had a presence about him that commanded attention. Their eyes met, and her brain seemed to stall. For a long moment, she seemed incapable of speech. She simply stared. And in that long moment, the horror of her surroundings retreated from her thoughts.

"My apologies for intruding at a difficult time, ma'am. I'm detective Adam Dawson – the investigating officer in this case. I just need to ask you a few questions."

"I'm not sure how much I can help you. I didn't see anything. I found her like this."

"No problem, ma'am." Adam smiled reassuringly. "Let's see what we can piece together, okay?"

Nodding hesitantly, Willow agreed.

"What is the victim's name?"

"Merida Davids."

"And what's your relationship to Ms Davids, ma'am?"

"She's my friend. She recently got out of a relationship and has been staying with me while she gets back on her feet."

Looking back over at Meri, she closed her eyes against a sharp pain in the region of her heart. Willow tried to breathe through the pain and panic. She couldn't envisage a life without Meri in it.

They'd been friends since nursery school. Their friendship had endured school, boyfriends, university, the craziness of youth – queuing for hours in the pouring rain for concert tickets, an urge to drink shots at three in the morning while belting show tunes at the top of their lungs.

She couldn't remember a time they hadn't been there for each other. It had even survived Meri's relationship with a man whose solution to everything was violence. Thankfully, it seemed JJ had finally managed to destroy their relationship beyond repair with his wild jealousy and violent temper.

"Was there a particular reason she left the relationship, Ms Martin? Or was it a case of it having run its course?" the detective asked.

"Her partner was abusive. He was always good at using his fists. If he had a point to make, a beating was his way of getting it across." Willow saw no need to beat around the bush.

She'd always feared one day his violent temper would result in one of those beatings being the death of Meri. But eventually, Meri came to her senses, leaving him when the last beating resulted in yet another hospital visit. When she discovered she was pregnant with JJ's twins, she'd voiced fears that if she didn't leave, it could very well end in tragedy. So, she'd packed her bags and moved in with Willow.

Willow was worried about Meri though. She loved having Meri living with her, but it hurt to watch her friend slip deeper and deeper into depression as time passed. Clearly, Meri missed JJ, but he was toxic for her.

"Do you have any idea when last Ms Davids had any contact with her ex-partner?"

"I'm not sure exactly, but I do know that since she moved in, he's been coming around to the house and phoning her constantly, begging her to come home."

It had concerned Willow. She could see JJ's constant presence was eroding Meri's hard-won resolve not to go back to him.

"When was the last time you saw Ms Davids?"

"We had breakfast together this morning before I left for work at around eight thirty. She wanted to know what she should make for dinner, as usual. Meri decided when she moved in that she would take care of the household duties while she stayed, as her way of making a contribution." Willow's voice hitched. "That was the last time I saw or spoke to her."

Tears trailed down her face as the realisation dawned that it might very well be the last thing she and Meri got to talk about ever again. She was very grateful to the big detective for giving her a moment when he handed her a handkerchief from his jacket pocket and said nothing more.

A sound behind her had that hypnotic gaze swinging away from him, effectively releasing him. His gaze shifting beyond her. He noticed the paramedics moving toward him.

As they wheeled the gurney past him, he a saw a young woman lying there. Nasty bruising was already visible, but underneath the vivid colouring, her skin was deathly pale. What snagged his attention was the enormous baby bump starkly highlighted by the white sheet covering her. It seemed today was his day for all the lousy cases. Stepping aside, he let the paramedics through on their way out to the ambulance.

Forensics passed the gurney at the front door. The same police officer who'd assisted Adam pointed them towards the living room, and they moved towards where he stood. The room behind him was in complete disarray, bearing testament to the fact that the victim on the gurney had clearly put up one hell of a fight. Sadly, it didn't seem as if it had done her any good. He knew the best way he could help this poor woman was to find out who had done this and bring them to justice.

· · ·

The metallic sound of the gurney being locked into place snagged her attention. She saw the paramedics wheeling Meri towards the door. Turning back to the detective, Willow spoke again.

"Forgive me, detective, I have to go with Meri now. I'm all she has left. I'll arrange with my neighbour, Ms Ellis, to come over. She'll lock up behind you."

"I understand, ma'am. It's no problem. I'll be in touch to follow up a little later then."

Thanking him, she headed for the foyer. As she collected the jacket she'd hung there what seemed like forever ago now, she made a quick call to her elderly neighbour to ask her to come over. Someone needed to be there while the police processed the crime scene – her home. She needed to be with Meri.

Ms Ellis, always so willing to help, promised to be right over.

Spotting the elderly lady coming up the drive as she reversed her car out, Willow stopped but left it idling as she got out to speak to her neighbour. With a hug and a heartfelt thank you, she climbed back into her car to follow the ambulance to the hospital. Beside herself with fear for her friend, Willow cried the entire drive to the hospital.

CHAPTER 2

In the short time, she'd been standing at Meri's bedside in the intensive care unit, Willow had come to despise the antiseptic smell and the mechanical sounds of the life support machines keeping her friend tethered to life. She hadn't thought they would let her stay the night with Meri as they weren't blood-related. But since she was pretty much all her friend had left in life, they allowed her in, feeling that her familiar presence would be soothing to the other woman.

Her heart ached as she looked down at the hideously injured woman lying in bed before her. Tears welled, yet again, streaking down her reddened cheeks. She'd cried so many tears already since she found her best friend lying on her living room floor, she thought there were no more left. Apparently, she was wrong.

She reached out and took Meri's hand in hers. It was icy cold. She lifted it to her cheek, cradling it gently as she tried to warm it. Through the tears, she looked down, silently willing Meri to open her eyes. She felt lost, adrift without her vibrant presence. There was never a dull moment when they were together. She would give almost anything to have Meri wake up. To see that enchanting smile of hers that always lit up the room and drew people to her.

A quiet clearing of a throat caused Willow to whip around. Standing behind her was the handsome man from the previous night. Not sure why she hadn't expected him to show up so soon, she stared at him blankly for a moment. So much had happened since then, she hadn't given him another thought. She was surprised she hadn't; he was most definitely memorable.

He had a handsome face saved from being beautiful by a rather nasty scar running from just in front of his left ear, curling around the bottom part of his cheek and disappearing under his chin. In a distant part of her mind, she wondered how badly it had hurt.

A strong, square jaw gave him a rather formidable appearance, but he had surprisingly full, soft-looking lips that went a long way to soften his face when he smiled. Intelligent eyes the colour of polished amber looked out from under straight eyebrows. And those eyes were focused squarely on her. Despite the dire circumstances, she couldn't help but feel a flutter of awareness in her stomach.

"I hope I'm not intruding?" the man enquired.

Giving him another once over, Willow tried to marshal her thoughts.

"No, it's fine," she finally answered. "I remember seeing you at the house last night. Do you have news?"

Willow watched in fascination as those lips quirked up in a brief smile.

"Apologies, ma'am. I don't. I have more questions, and I need to take down a written statement from you."

The detective, Adam, she recalled belatedly stuck his hand out in greeting. Willow hesitated a moment but took it eventually. She stilled as electricity raced up her arm. Pulling her tingling hand away from his, she returned his smile with an uncertain one of her own.

"What more can I tell you?"

"Ms Martin, there are a couple of points you spoke about last night I'd like to follow up on. I was wondering if you perhaps have some time now?"

"To be honest, like I mentioned last night, I really don't know much. I'm not sure how I can be of any further help. As I said, that's how I found her when I got home. It won't surprise me if JJ is involved in this though. This is exactly his style."

"I'm interested in a bit of background regarding Ms Davids. There might very well be something there that will point this investigation in the right direction. Based on how well you know Ms Davids."

"Yes, Meri and I have been best friends since we were about five."

"Could I steal you away for a few minutes? Maybe chat at the coffee shop? That way if you're needed, they can call you, and you'll be able to get back here quickly." At her nod of assent, Adam gestured for her to precede him from the room to the elevators.

Willow took a seat at a table while Adam went to get their coffee at the counter. She took the time to study him, again marvelling at how comfortable she felt in his company despite not knowing him at all. Not having much exposure to male company growing up, she wasn't usually at ease being around men other than her brother. At least not until she got to know them. He just seemed to give off "trust me" vibes.

Adam returned to the table with their coffee, cutting her reverie short. Sitting down opposite her, he took a notebook and pen from the inside pocket of his sports jacket. Willow found herself surprised at how much information he'd already gathered. Clearly, he'd been busy since last night. The questions were astute and well-honed, digging for maximum knowledge to get a sharply accurate picture.

Willow wasn't sure if it was the stress of the last twenty-four hours, or that she felt at ease with the detective, but she found the words just tumbling out, sharing with him all the things that had plagued her about JJ all these years. She shared about his violent temper and all the times it had led to Meri being rushed to the hospital. How it had always been her greatest fear that one of the beatings JJ gave Meri would eventually lead to her friend's demise. She even told him of her suspicions – that despite a lack of evidence, she was convinced that JJ was the person responsible for this one too.

Eventually, Willow's outburst wound down. For a moment, she felt embarrassed to have ranted like that. But she also felt lighter for having finally gotten all of it off her chest. They were nearly done, with just a couple more questions to go, when Willow's cell phone rang, and she recognised the hospital's number.

"Oh God, Meri!" was all she said as she whirled out of her chair and sprinted for the stairs, in too much of a rush to wait for the elevator.

Adam followed her quickly, skidding to a halt at the nurses' station to see Willow huddled over to the side, staying well out of the way as the staff worked on reviving her friend. The machines Meri was attached to beeped, hissed, and jangled as they worked valiantly and fought desperately to keep her alive.

Willow was ashen and her eyes enormous as she stared at the chaos before her. The pain and horror etched on her beautiful face had him clenching his hands in impotent fury. He had no way to change what had been done and no way to comfort her in the face of a rather inevitable outcome. Nobody was saying it, but he'd borne witness to too many scenes like this one to believe there'd be a happy ending to this regretable story.

Suddenly, the group around the bed parted as the nurse at the head began to wheel the bed towards the door. Another nurse went over to speak to Willow. As the other nurses rushed past him, he heard the words "operating theatre three, premature labour, and haemorrhaging" uttered. Looking back over, he saw the nurse holding Willow's hand, still talking to her. As if the news the nurse was sharing with her was a burden too heavy to bear, Willow sank to the floor sobbing like her heart was breaking.

Walking over to the nurse, he indicated he'd take it from there. Grateful, she gave him a sad, tired smile and left them to it. He sank down beside Willow on the floor. After a brief internal battle, he placed an awkward arm around Willow's shoulders. They sat like that until she finally cried herself out. Then they sat in silence as they waited for news.

*If you'd like to read more of Adam and Willow's story, you can find it **here**.*

ABOUT THE AUTHOR

International bestselling author Dorothy Ewels lives in the city of her birth, Cape Town, South Africa, with her husband, son, two crazy rescue dogs and a cat with plenty of cattitude. A lifelong love affair with reading got her writing at a young age, but it wasn't until she was retrenched in 2017 that she finally found the courage to write her first book, leading to its publication in 2018. She's addicted to coffee, books and finding humor in life, not to mention happy endings against all odds. As well as being a proud and active member of the Romance Writer's Organization of South Africa (ROSA), Dorothy is also thrilled to be a contributing author in Samantha A. Cole's Suspenseful Seduction World, Vi Keeland and Penelope Ward's Cocky Hero Club and Susan Stoker's Special Forces.

WHERE TO FIND THE AUTHOR

ALSO BY THE AUTHOR

Links to all these books can be found on

www.dorothyewels.co.za/my-books, for all platforms

Love at Last

Destined

A Cowboy for Christmas

My Girl

Meet Me Halfway

Suspenseful Seduction World

Trusting Laurence

Liberating Mia

Cooper's Salvation

Cocky Hero Club

Sassy Surrogate

Special Forces: Operation Alpha

Operation Checkmate

Knight's Queen

Lucky in Love

Baring All

Dutch's Defense

Scooter's Endgame – releasing September 12, 2023

Gator's Gambit – releasing November 2023

Digit's Deflection – releasing January 2024

New series launching in Susan Stoker's Special Forces World 2025
Meeting Leila – *short story only available to newsletter subscribers*
Loving Leila – release date to be advised

Audio

Sassy Surrogate